Bantam Books by Barbara Cartland
Ask your bookseller for the books you have missed

1 The Daring Deception
4 Lessons in Love
6 The Bored Bridegroom
8 The Dangerous Dandy
10 The Wicked Marquis
11 The Castle of Fear
14 The Karma of Love
21 The Tears of Love
22 A Very Naughty Angel
24 The Devil in Love
25 As Eagles Fly
27 Say Yes, Samantha
28 The Cruel Count
29 The Mask of Love
30 Blood on the Snow
31 An Arrow of Love
33 A Kiss for the King
34 A Frame of Dreams
35 The Fragrant Flower
36 The Elusive Earl
38 The Golden Illusion
43 An Angel in Hell
44 The Wild Cry of Love
45 The Blue-Eyed Witch
46 The Incredible
   Honeymoon
47 A Dream from the Night
48 Conquered by Love
49 Never Laugh at Love
50 The Secret of the Glen
52 Hungry for Love

54 The Dream and the Glory
55 The Taming of Lady
   Lorinda
56 The Disgraceful Duke
57 Vote for Love
61 A Rhapsody of Love
.62 The Marquis Who Hated
   Women
63 Look, Listen and Love
64 A Duel with Destiny
65 The Curse of the Clan
66 Punishment of a Vixen
67 The Outrageous Lady
68 A Touch of Love
69 The Dragon and the Pearl
70 The Love Pirate
71 The Temptation of Torilla
72 Love and the Loathsome
   Leopard
73 The Naked Battle
74 The Hell-Cat and the King
75 No Escape from Love
76 The Castle Made for Love
77 The Sign of Love
78 The Saint and the Sinner
79 A Fugitive from Love
80 The Twists and Turns of
   Love
81 The Problems of Love
82 Love Leaves at Midnight
83 Magic or Mirage

Barbara Cartland's Library of Love

2 His Hour
3 The Knave of Diamonds
4 A Safety Match
5 The Hundredth Chance
6 The Reason Why
7 The Way of an Eagle
8 The Vicissitudes of
   Evangeline
9 The Bars of Iron

10 Man and Maid
11 The Sons of the Sheik
12 Six Days
13 Rainbow in the Spray
14 The Great Moment
15 Greatheart
16 The Broad Highway
17 The Sequence

Barbara Cartland's Library of Love
The Broad Highway
by Jeffrey Farnol

Condensed by Barbara Cartland

BANTAM BOOKS
TORONTO · NEW YORK · LONDON

THE BROAD HIGHWAY
A Bantam Book / April 1978

ISBN 0-553-11468-9

Published simultaneously in the United States and Canada

Bantam Books are published by Bantam Books, Inc. Its trade-
mark, consisting of the words "Bantam Books" and the por-
trayal of a bantam, is registered in the United States Patent
Office and in other countries. Marca Registrada. Bantam
Books, Inc., 666 Fifth Avenue, New York, New York 10019.

PRINTED IN THE UNITED STATES OF AMERICA

Introduction
by
Barbara Cartland

This is one of the first novels I ever read. I loved it and it was the same for many of my generation. The story is both idealistic and exciting, and there was never a more alluring heroine than Charmian, a more gallant hero than Peter, a more villainous villain than his cousin Sir Maurice Vibart.

This is real romance and one is swept into a world of deeds of valour and love from the first word to the last.

Chapter
One

" 'And to my nephew Maurice Vibart I bequeath the sum of twenty thousand pounds in the fervent hope that it may help him to the devil within the year, or as soon after as may be.' "

Here Mr. Grainger paused in his reading to glance up over the rim of his spectacles, while Sir Richard lay back in his chair and laughed.

"God! I'd give a hundred pounds if he could have been present to hear that!"

Mr. Grainger, dignified and solemn, coughed a short, dry cough behind his hand.

"Help him to the devil within the year," repeated Sir Richard, still chuckling.

"Pray proceed, Sir," I said.

But instead of complying Mr. Grainger laid down the parchment.

"You are, I believe, unacquainted with your cousin, Sir Maurice Vibart?" he enquired.

1

"I have never seen him," I said, "but I have frequently heard mention of him nevertheless."

"Egad!" cried Sir Richard. "Who hasn't heard of Buck Vibart—beat Ted Jarraway of Swansea in five rounds—drove a coach and four down Whitehall on the sidewalk—ran away with a French Marquise while but a boy of twenty, and shot her husband into the bargain.

"Devilish celebrated figure in 'sporting circles,' friend of the Prince Regent . . ."

"So I understand," I said.

"Altogether as complete a young blackguard as ever swaggered down St. James's."

"His debts," said Mr. Grainger, "are very heavy, I believe."

"Then doubtless some arrangement can be made to— But continue your reading, please," I replied.

" 'Furthermore, to my nephew Peter Vibart, cousin to the above, I will and bequeath my blessing and the sum of ten guineas in cash.' "

"Good God!" cried Sir Richard, leaping to his feet. "The man must have been mad. Ten guineas—why, it's an insult—you'll never take it, of course, Peter."

"On the contrary, Sir." I said.

"But—ten guineas!" bellowed the Baronet. "On my soul now, George was a cold-blooded fish, but I didn't think even he was capable of such a despicable trick. Why, it would have been kinder to have left you nothing at all—but it was like George—bitter to the end—ten guineas!"

"Is ten guineas," I replied, "and when one comes to think of it, much may be done with ten guineas."

Sir Richard grew purple in the face, but before he could speak Mr. Grainger began to read again:

" 'Moreover, the sum of five hundred thousand pounds, now vested in the funds, shall be paid to either Maurice or Peter Vibart, aforesaid, if either shall, within one calendar year, become the husband of the Lady Sophia Sefton of Cambourne.' "

"Good God!" exclaimed Sir Richard.

" 'Failing which,' " read Mr. Grainger, " 'the said sum, namely, five hundred thousand pounds, shall be bestowed upon such charity or charities as the trustees shall select. Signed by me, this tenth day of April, eighteen hundred and—— *George Vibart*. Duly Witnessed by *Adam Penfleet, Martha Trent.*' "

"And that is all?" I enquired at last.

"That," said Mr. Grainger, not looking at me now, "is all."

"The Lady Sophia," murmured Sir Richard as if to himself, "the Lady Sophia!"

Then, stopping suddenly before me in his walk, "Oh, Peter!" he said, clapping his hand down upon my shoulder. "Oh, Peter, that settles it, you're done for—a crueller will was never made."

"The Lady Sophia Sefton of Cambourne!" I said, rubbing my chin.

"Why, that's just it," roared the Baronet; "she's a reigning toast—most famous beauty in the country. London's mad over her—she can pick and choose from all the finest gentlemen in England. Oh, it's 'good-bye' to all your hopes of the inheritance, Peter, and that's the devil of it."

"Sir, I fail to see your argument," I replied.

"What?" cried Sir Richard, facing round on me. "D'you think you'd have a chance with her then?"

"Why not?"

"Without friends, position, or money? Pish, boy! I tell you that every Buck and Dandy—every mincing Macaroni in the three kingdoms—would give his very legs to marry her—either for her beauty or her fortune.

"And let me inform you further that she's devilish high and haughty with it all—they do say she even rebuffed the Prince Regent himself."

"But then, Sir, I consider myself a better man than the Prince Regent," I said, "and referring to the Lady Sophia, I have heard that she once galloped her horse up the steps of Saint Paul's Cathedral. . . ."

"And down again, Peter," added Sir Richard.

"Also, she is said to have a temper, and is above average height, I believe, and I have a nat-

4

ural antipathy to termagants, more especially tall ones."

"Termagant!" cried Sir Richard. "Why, she's the handsomest woman in London. She's none of your milk-and-watery, meek-mouthed misses—curse me, no! She's all fire and blood and high mettle—a woman—a glorious, divine, black-browed goddess—a positive plum!"

"Sir Richard," I said, "should I ever contemplate marriage, which is most improbable, my wife must be sweet and shy, with a soft voice, instead of your bold, strong-armed, horse-galloping creature; above all, she must be sweet and clinging. . . ."

"Sweet and sticky! Listen to him, Grainger. Just one glance of the glorious Sefton's bright eyes, one glance only, Grainger, and he'd be at her feet—on his knees—on his confounded knees, Sir!"

"The question is, how do you propose to maintain yourself in the future?" Mr. Grainger said at this point. "Life under your altered fortunes must prove necessarily hard, Mr. Peter."

He paused, then continued:

"I have been wondering if you would care to accept a position in my office. The remuneration would be small at first and quite insignificant in comparison to the income you have been receiving."

"But it would be money earned," I replied,

"which is infinitely preferable to that for which we never turn a hand—at least I think so."

"Then you accept?"

"No, Sir," I said, "though I am grateful to you, and thank you most sincerely for your offer, but I have never felt the least inclination to the practise of law."

"And pray," Sir Richard said, "what do you propose to do with yourself?"

"I shall go, Sir, on a walking tour through Kent and Surrey and into Devonshire and then probably to Cornwall."

"With a miserable ten guineas in your pocket? Preposterous—absurd!" Sir Richard retorted.

"Referring to your proposed tour, Mr. Peter, when do you expect to start?" asked Grainger.

"Early tomorrow morning, Sir."

"I will not attempt to dissuade you, well knowing the difficulty," he said with a faint smile, "but a letter addressed to me at Lincoln's Inn will always find me and receive my immediate attention."

Then he rose, bowed, and, having shaken my hand, left the room and closed the door behind him.

"Peter," exclaimed the Baronet, striding up and down, "Peter, you are a fool—a hot-headed, self-sufficient, pragmatical young fool!"

"I am sorry you should think so," I answered.

"And," he continued, regarding me with a defiant stare, "I shall expect you to draw upon me for any sum that—that you may require for the present—friendship's sake and—and all that sort of thing, and—er—oh, damme, you understand, Peter?"

"Sir Richard," I said, grasping his unwilling hand, "I thank you from the bottom of my heart."

"Pooh, Peter, dammit!" he said, snatching his hand away and thrusting it hurriedly into his pocket, farther out of reach.

At this moment, with a discreet knock, the butler appeared to announce that Sir Richard's horse was waiting. The Baronet somewhat hastily caught up his hat and gloves, and I followed him out of the house and down the steps.

"Peter," he said, very slowly and heavily, "I'm growing old, and I shall never marry—and sometimes of an evening I get very lonely, very lonely, Peter."

He stopped for a while, gazing away towards the green slopes of distant Shooter's Hill.

"Oh!" he said at last. "Won't you come to the Hall and help me to spend my money?"

"Sir Richard," I said at last, "wherever I go I shall treasure the recollection of this moment, but . . ."

"Oh, dammit!" Sir Richard exclaimed, and spurred on his horse. Yet once he turned in his saddle to flourish his whip to me before he galloped out of sight.

So I set off.

* * *

That day I passed through several villages, stopping only to eat and drink, and evening was falling as, having left Sevenoaks behind, I came to the brow of a certain hill, a long and very steep descent which is called the River Hill.

Here, rising stark against the evening sky, was a gibbet, and standing beneath it a man—a short, square man in a shabby bottle-green coat, with a wide-brimmed beaver hat sloped down over his eyes.

He stood with his feet well apart while he stared up at that which dangled by a stout chain from the cross-beam of the gibbet, something black and shrivelled and horrible that had once been human.

As I came up, the man touched the brim of his hat in salutation.

"It's a horrible sight," I said.

"It is." The man nodded. "It's a sight to turn a man's stomach, that is!"

"You knew him, perhaps?" I asked.

"Knew him," repeated the man, staring at me over his shoulder, "knew him—ah—that is, I knew of him."

"A highwayman?"

"Nick Scrope his name was," answered the

man with a nod, "hung at Maidstone assizes last year; and here he is hanged in chains as a warning to all and sundry."

"What?" I said. "Do you think for one moment that such a sight, horrible though it is, could possibly deter a man from robbery or murder whose mind is already made up to it?"

Once more, though my whole being revolted at the sight, I turned to look at the tall black shaft of the gibbet, and from this back again to my companion, to find him regarding me with a curious twisted smile, and a long-barrelled pistol within a foot of my head.

"Well?" I said, staring.

"Sir," he said, tapping his boot with his stick, "I must trouble you for your watch and any small change you may have."

For a moment I hesitated, glancing from his grinning mouth swiftly over the deserted road and back again.

"Also," the fellow said, "I must ask you to be sharp about it."

It was with very clumsy fingers that I drew the watch from my fob and passed it to him.

"Now your pockets," he suggested. "Turn 'em out."

Reluctantly I obeyed and brought out the ten guineas, which he pocketed; and two pennies —which he bade me keep.

"For," he said, "it will buy you a draught of ale, Sir, and there's good stuff to be had at the

White Hart, and there's nothing like a draught of good ale to comfort a man in such small adversity like this."

He broke off suddenly, for from somewhere below us on the hill came the unmistakable sound of wheels. Quickly and nimbly the man ran across the road, turned, nodded, and vanished among the trees and underbrush that clothed the steep slope down to the valley below, leaving me alone.

Walking down the hill to the White Hart Inn, I sat down and with one of my last two pennies ordered a tankard of ale.

* * *

I was presently aroused by a loud, rough voice. I raised my eyes and fixed them on the speaker.

He was a square-shouldered, bullet-headed fellow, and I noticed that whenever he spoke the others held their peace and hung upon every word.

"Yes, Sirs, says I," he began, louder than before, and with a flourish of his long-stemmed pipe, "yes, Sirs, Tom Cragg's my name and craggy's my nature."

"Tom," cried a one-eyed man, "wot's all this we heared of Ted Jarraway of Swansea bein' knocked out in five rounds by this 'ere Lord Vibbot up in London?"

"If you was to ask me who put Ted Jarraway

to sleep, I should answer you Sir Maurice Vibart, commonly called Buck Vibart; an' it took ten rounds to do it, not five."

At the mention of my cousin's name I pricked up my ears.

"And what's all this 'bout him 'putting out' Tom Cragg in three?"

At this there was a sudden silence.

"I says," cried Tom Cragg, flourishing a great fist in the air, "I says as 'e done it—on a foul!

"A golden guinea to the man as can stand on 'is pins an' fight me for five minutes—an' as for Buck Vibart—curse 'im, I say, as 'e won on a foul!"

'A guinea,' I thought to myself, 'is a fortune!' And setting down my empty tankard I crossed the room and touched Cragg upon the shoulder.

"I will fight you," I said, "for a guinea."

As he looked at me his mouth fell open and he backed away!

"You?" he said, recovering himself with an effort. "You?"

He paused, then went on slowly:

"If—if I said anything against you-know-who, I'm sorry for it—me 'aving the greatest respec' for you-know-who. You understand me, I think."

Then he winked three separate, distinct times.

"No, I don't understand you in the least," I replied. "All that I care about is the guinea in question."

"Can't be done," Cragg said, shaking his head, "leastways—not 'ere."

"I'm not particular," I said. "If you prefer, we might manage it very well in the stable with a couple of lanthorns."

So the landlord called for lanthorns and led the way to a large out-building at the back of the Inn, into which we all trooped.

"It seems to be a good place and very suitable. If Tom Cragg is ready," I said, turning up the wrist-bands of my shirt, "why, so am I."

But Tom Cragg was gone as completely as though he had melted into thin air, and with him all my hopes of winning the guinea and a comfortable bed.

"If," I said, glancing round the ring of faces, "there is any man here who is at all willing to fight for a guinea, or ten shillings, or even five, I should be very glad of the chance to earn it."

But seeing how each held his peace, I sighed, and turning my back upon them set off along the darkening road.

* * *

As I approached the brow of the hill I suddenly remembered that I must once more pass the gibbet. I was almost abreast of it when a figure rose from beneath it and slouched into the road to meet me. I stopped there and then, grasping my heavy staff, waiting its approach.

"Be that you, Sir?"

I recognised the voice of Tom Cragg.

"And what do you want with me?"

"I 'opes as theer's no offence, My Lord. But I know when I'm beat. I knowed ye as soon as I laid eyes on ye, an' if I said as it were a foul, why, there was no offence, My Lord. I know you an' you know me."

"But I don't know you," I answered, "and for that matter, neither do you know me."

"Why, you ain't got no whiskers, My Lord—leastways not now, but . . ."

"And what the devil has that got to do with it?" I said angrily.

"Disguises, p'raps! After that kidnappin', an' me 'avin' laid out Sir Jasper Trent, in Wyeth Street—accordin' to your orders, My Lord—the Prince give me word to clear out—cut an' run for it till it blowed over; an' I thought p'raps, knowin' as you an' 'im 'ad 'ad words, I thought as you 'ad cut and run for it too. . . ."

"And I think that you are drunk. If you still wish to fight, put up your hands; if not, get out of my road."

He removed his hat and stood there staring and scratching his head in perplexity.

"I seen many rum goes in my time," he said, "but I never see so rummy a go as this 'ere!"

So I left him and strode on down the hill.

Looking back, I saw him standing where I had left him beneath the gibbet, still scratching his head, and staring after me.

Chapter
Two

Sometime later, I sat in the old Cock Tavern.

After a delicious meal of ham and eggs, served to me by a charming young girl, I sat with a contented mind, smoking my pipe and staring out at the falling summer rain.

And presently, chancing to turn my eyes up the road, I watched the rapid approach of a chaise.

The postillion swung his horses towards the Inn and a moment later pulled up before the door.

The chaise door was thrown open and three gentlemen alighted. The first was short, bull-necked, and loud of voice. The second was a tall, languid gentleman, who carried a flat, oblong box beneath one arm. He paused to fondle his whiskers, and looked up at the Inn with an exaggerated air of disgust. The third stood mutely by, his hands thrust into the pockets of his greatcoat, and stared straight before him.

The three of them entered the room together, and, while the languid gentleman paused to survey himself in the small, cracked mirror that hung against the wall, the short individual bustled to the fire and spread out his hands to the blaze.

"A good half-hour before our time," he said, glancing towards the third gentleman, who stood looking out the window, his hands still deep in his pockets. "We did the last ten miles well under the hour—come, what do you say to a glass of brandy?"

At this his languid companion turned from the mirror, and I noticed that he too glanced at the silent figure by the window.

"By all means," he said, "though Sir Jasper would hardly seem in a drinking humour."

With the very slightest shrug of his shoulders he turned back to the mirror again.

"No, Mr. Chester, I am not—in a drinking humour," answered Sir Jasper, without turning round or taking his eyes from the window.

'Sir Jasper . . . ?' I wondered to myself. 'Now where, and in what connection, have I heard such a name before?'

He was of a slight build, and seemingly younger than either of his companions, by some years, but what struck me particularly about him was the extreme pallor of his face.

I noticed also a peculiar habit he had of moistening his lips at frequent intervals with the tip of his tongue, and there was, besides, something in the way he stared at the trees, the wet road, and the grey sky—a strange, wide-eyed intensity that drew and held my attention.

"Devilish weather—devilish, on my life and soul!" exclaimed the short, red-faced man in a loud, peevish tone. "Hot one day, cold the next, now sun, now rain. Now in France—ah, what a climate—heavenly—positively divine!"

"Selby," Sir Jasper said in the same repressed tone, and still without taking his eyes from the grey prospect of sky and tree and winding road, "there is no fairer land in all the world than this England of ours; it is a good thing to die for England—but that is a happiness reserved for comparatively few."

And with the words he sighed a strange, fluttering sigh, and thrust his hands deeper into his pockets.

"Die!" repeated the man Selby, in a loud, boisterous way. "Who talks of death?"

"Deuced unpleasant subject!" said the other, with a shrug at the cracked mirror. "Something so infernally cold and clammy about it—like the weather."

"And yet it will be a glorious day later. The clouds are thinning already," Sir Jasper went on. "Strange, but I never realised until this morning how green—and wonderful—everything is!"

The languid Mr. Chester forgot the mirror, and turned to stare at Sir Jasper's back, with raised brows, while the man Selby shook his head and smiled unpleasantly.

As he did so, his eye encountered me, where I sat quietly in my corner, and his thick brows twitched sharply together in a frown.

"In an hour's time, gentlemen," pursued Sir Jasper, "we shall write *finis* to a more or less interesting incident, and I beg of you, in that hour, to remember my prophecy—that it will be a glorious day later."

Mr. Chester filled a glass and, crossing to the speaker, tendered it to him.

"Come," said Mr. Chester persuasively. "Just a bracer!"

Sir Jasper shook his head, but next moment reached out a white, unsteady hand, and raised the brandy to his lips; yet as he drank, I saw the spirit slop over and trickle from his chin.

"Thanks, Chester," said he, returning the empty glass. "Is it time we started yet?"

"It's just half-past seven," answered Mr. Chester, consulting his watch, "and I'm rather hazy as to the exact place."

"Deepdene Wood," said Sir Jasper dreamily. "You know the place?"

"Oh yes!"

"Then we may as well start, if you are ready?"

"Yes. And it will be cool and fresh outside."

17

"Settle the bill, Selby, we'll walk on slowly," said Mr. Chester, and, with a last glance at the mirror, he slipped his arm within Sir Jasper's and they went out together.

Mr. Selby, meanwhile, rang for the bill, frowning at me all the time.

"What the devil are you staring at?" he demanded suddenly in a loud, bullying tone.

"If you are pleased to refer to me, Sir," I said, "I would say that my eyes were given for use, and that having used them upon you I have long since arrived at the conclusion that I don't like you."

"An impertinent young jackanapes!" he said. "Damnation, I think I'll pull your nose!"

"Why, you may try, and welcome, Sir," I said, "though I should advise you not, for should you make the attempt I should be compelled to throw you out the window."

At this moment the pretty maid appeared and tendered him the bill with a curtsey. He glanced at it, tossed some money upon the table, and turned to stare at me again.

"If ever I meet you again . . ." he began.

"You'd probably know me," I put in.

"Without a doubt," he answered, putting on his hat, "and should you stare at me with those damned impertinent eyes of yours, I should, most certainly, pull your nose for you—on the spot, Sir."

"And I should as certainly throw you out the window!"

"An impertinent young jackanapes!" he said again, and went out, banging the door behind him.

Glancing from the window, I saw him catch up with the other two, and all three walked on together down the road. Sir Jasper was in the middle, and I noticed that his hands were still deep in his pockets.

Now, as I watched their forms getting smaller and smaller in the distance, there grew upon me a feeling that he who walked between would never more come walking back.

In a little while, I called for and settled my score which I paid with the money I had earned heaving bales. The pretty chamber maid helped me with my knapsack.

"By the way," I said, pausing upon the worn steps and looking back at her, "how far is it to Deepdene Wood?"

❊   ❊   ❊

Some half-mile along the road was a stile, and beyond the stile a path that led away over field and meadow and winding stream to the blue verge of distant woods.

Midway between these woods and the place where I stood, there moved three figures, and, far away though they were, I could still make out that the middle one walked with his hands—those tremulous, betraying hands—thrust deep within his pockets.

"Sir Jasper!" I said to myself.

Somewhere in the background of my consciousness I had a vague recollection of having heard mention of such a name before, but exactly when and where I could not for the life of me remember.

"Sir Jasper!" I said to myself again. "It is a very uncommon name, and should be easy to recollect."

I had often prided myself on possessing a singularly retentive memory, especially for names and faces, but the more I pondered the matter, the more hazy I became. So I walked on through the sweet, wet grass, racking my brain for a solution to the problem, but finding none.

When I again looked up, the three figures had vanished where the path took a sharp bend round a clump of pollard oaks, and, determined not to lose them, I hurried my steps; but when I in turn rounded the corner, not a soul was in sight.

Wondering, I hastened forward, and then, happening to look through the hedge, which grew very thick and high, I stopped all at once.

On the other side of the hedge was a strip of meadow bounded by a brook; across this stream was a small rustic bridge, and on this bridge was a man.

Midway between this man and myself stood a group of four gentlemen, all talking very earnestly together, while somewhat apart from these, his head bent, his hands still thrust deep in his pockets, stood Sir Jasper.

And from him my eyes wandered to the man upon the bridge—a tall, broad-shouldered fellow, in a buff-coloured greatcoat, who whistled to himself, and stared down into the stream, swinging his tasselled riding-boot to and fro.

All at once, as if in response to some signal, he rose, unbuttoned his coat, drew it off, and flung it across the handrail of the bridge.

Mr. Chester was on his knees before the oblong box, and I saw the glint of the pistols as he handed them up. The distance had already been paced and marked out, and now each man took his ground.

Sir Jasper, still in his greatcoat, his hat over his eyes, his neckerchief loose and dangling, one hand in his pocket, the other grasping his weapon; his antagonist, on the contrary, jaunty and debonaire, a dandy from the crown of his hat to the soles of his shining boots.

Their arms were raised almost together.

The man Selby glanced from one to the other, a handkerchief fluttered, fell, and in that instant came the report of a pistol.

I saw Sir Jasper reel backwards, steady himself, and fire in return; then, while the blue smoke yet hung in the still air, he staggered blindly and fell.

Mr. Chester, and two or three more, ran forward and knelt beside him, while his opponent shrugged his shoulders and, taking off his hat, pointed out the bullet hole to his white-faced second.

And in a little while they lifted Sir Jasper in their arms, but seeing how his head hung, a sudden sickness came upon me, for I knew indeed that he would go walking back nevertheless.

Yet his eyes were wide and staring—staring up at the blue heaven with the same fixed intensity as they had done at the Inn.

Then I too looked up at the cloudless sky, and round upon the fair earth; and in that moment I for one remembered his prophecy of an hour ago. And indeed the day was glorious.

* * *

Following the high road, I came, in a little, to where the ways divided.

At the parting of the ways was a finger-post with the words: TO LONDON. TO TONBRIDGE WELLS. TO PEMBRY.

Now as I stood beneath the finger-post, debating which road I should take, I was aware of the sound of wheels, and glancing about saw a carrier's cart approaching.

"If so be you are for Pembry, or thereabouts,

Sir," he said, bringing his horses to a standstill, "why, jump up, Sir—that is, if you be so minded."

"My course lies anywhere," I said.

"Then, Sir, jump up," he said.

So I climbed up on the seat beside him, and we jogged along for several miles, engaged in pleasant conversation.

After a while I asked:

"You never heard of Tom Cragg, did you?"

"Can't say as I have," he answered, stroking his chin thoughtfully.

"And you don't know who 'George' is, of course?" I continued musingly.

"Why, I've knowed a many Georges in my time," he said, "and then there's George, Prince o' Wales, the Prince Regent, as they calls him now."

"George, Prince of Wales!" I said, staring. "By heavens, Tom, I believe you've hit it!"

I sprang down from the cart.

"My cottage is nearby, Sir, and I shall be proud for you to eat supper wi' me—that is, if you be so minded."

"Many thanks," I replied, "but I am not so minded, and so good-bye!"

With the words, I wrung his honest hand in mine and went upon my way.

"George, Prince of Wales!" I said to myself. "Could this be the 'George' they had meant? If so, then who and what had they supposed me?"

Hereupon, as I walked, I fell into a profound meditation in which I presently remembered how that Tom Cragg had also mentioned the Prince, giving me to understand that His Highness had actually ordered him (Tom Cragg) to leave London; and why?

"Arter that theer kidnappin', an' me 'avin' laid out Sir Jasper Trant—accordin' to yer order."

Sir Jasper Trent! I stopped stock still in the road. Sir Jasper Trent! At last I remembered the name that had eluded me so persistently. Remembered it? Nay, indeed it was rather as if the Pugilist had whispered the words into my ear, and I glanced round almost expecting to see him.

"After that theer kidnappin', an' me 'avin' laid out Sir Jasper Trent—accordin' to yer orders!"

According to my orders, or rather the orders of the man for whom he (in common with the two gentlemen at the Chequers) had mistaken me. But who was that man?

Of him I knew two facts—namely, that he was much like me in person, and had formerly worn, or possibly still wore, whiskers.

Beyond these two facts I could get no further, revolve the matter how I might, so I presently shrugged my shoulders, and banishing it from my thoughts, for the time being, set forward at a good pace.

* * *

The sun was already sinking when I came to a pump beside the way. Seizing the handle, I worked it vigorously, then drank and pumped alternately until I had quenched my thirst.

I now found myself prodigiously hungry, and, remembering the bread and cheese in my knapsack, looked about for an inviting spot in which to eat.

On one side of the road was a thick hedge, and beneath this hedge was a deep, dry, grassy ditch; there I sat down, took out the loaf and the cheese, and, opening my clasp knife, prepared to fall to.

At that moment, hearing a rustling close by, I looked up straight into a face that was protruded through a gap in the hedge above me.

I needed but a glance at the battered hat with its jaunty brim and great silver buckle, and the haggard, devil-may-care face below, to recognise an individual whom I had seen at the tavern that very morning.

It was a very thin face, pale, and hollow-eyed, and framed in black curly hair whose very blackness did but accentuate the extreme pallor of the skin, which was tight and drawn above the cheek bones and angle of the jaw.

Yet, as I looked at this face, worn and cadaverous though it was, in the glance of the hollow eyes and in the line of the clean-cut mouth I saw that mysterious something which marks a man, what we call for want of a better word a "gentleman."

"Good-evening!" he said, and lifted the battered hat.

"Good-evening," I returned.

"Pardon me," he said, "but I was saluting the bread and cheese."

"Indeed," I said.

"Indeed!" he rejoined. "It is the first edible I have been on speaking terms with, so to speak, for rather more than three days, Sir."

"You are probably hungry," I said.

"It would be foolish to deny it, Sir."

"Then, if you care to eat with me in the ditch here, you are heartily welcome," I said.

"With all the pleasure in life!" he said, vaulting very nimbly through the hedge. "Believe me, I . . ." There he stopped, very suddenly, and stood looking at me.

"Ah!" he said gently, and with a rising inflection, letting the ejaculation escape in a long-drawn breath.

"Well?" I enquired.

Now as I looked up at him, the whole aspect of the man, from the toes of his broken boots to the crown of the battered hat seemed to undergo a change, as though a sudden, fierce anger had leapt into life, and been controlled, but by a strong effort.

"On my life and soul, now!" he said, falling back a step and eyeing me with a vaguely unpleasant smile. "This is most unexpected—a most unlooked-for pleasure, it is—I vow it is."

"You flatter me," I said.

"No, Sir, no; to meet you again—someday —somewhere—alone—quite alone, Sir, is a pleasure I have frequently dwelt upon but never hoped to realise. Do me the infinite kindness to stand up."

"Sir," I answered, cutting a slice from the loaf, "you are the third person within the last forty-eight hours who has mistaken me for another; it really gets quite wearisome."

"Mistaken you?" he broke in, and his smile grew suddenly bitter. "Do you think it possible that I could ever mistake you?"

"I am sure of it!" I said. "Still, in this instance, never having seen your face or heard your voice until today, I shall continue to sit here and eat my bread and cheese, and if you are wise you will hasten to follow my so excellent example while there is any left, for I warn you, I am mightily hungry."

"Come, come," he said, advancing upon me threateningly, "enough of this foolery!"

"By all means," I said, "sit down, like a sensible fellow, and tell me for whom you mistake me."

"Sir, with all the pleasure in life!" he said, clenching his fists, and I saw his nostrils dilate suddenly. "I take you for the greatest rogue, the most gentlemanly rascal but one in all England!"

"Yes," I said, "and my name?"

"Sir Maurice Vibart!"

"Sir Maurice Vibart?" I sprang to my feet, staring at him in amazement. "Sir Maurice Vibart is my cousin."

And so we stood for a long minute, immobile and silent, eyeing each other above the bread and cheese.

"Sir," said my companion at last, lifting the battered hat, "I tender you my apology, and I shall be delighted to eat with you in the ditch, if you are in the same mind about it."

"Then you believe me?"

"Indubitably, Sir," he answered with a faint smile. "Had you indeed been Sir Maurice, either he or I, and most probably I, would be lying flat in the road by this."

So without more ado we sat down in the ditch together, side by side, and began to eat.

And now I noticed that when he thought my eye was upon him, my companion ate with a due deliberation and nicety, and when he thought it was off, with a voracity that was painful to witness. And after we had eaten awhile in silence, he turned to me with a sigh.

"This is very excellent cheese!" he said.

"Hunger is a fine sauce," I replied, "and you are probably hungry."

"Hungry!" he repeated, bolting a mouthful and knocking his hat over his eyes with a slap on its dusty crown. "Egad, Mr. Vibart! So

would you be—so would any man be who has
lived on anything he could beg, borrow, or steal,
with an occasional meal of turnips—hungry—oh,
damme!"

And after a while, when there remained
nothing of loaf and cheese save a few scattered
crumbs, my companion leaned back and gave another sigh.

"Sir," he said, with an airy wave of the hand,
"in me you behold a highly promising young gentleman ruined by a most implacable enemy—himself, Sir. In the first place, you must know my
name is Beverley ..."

"Beverley?" I repeated.

"Beverley," he said, and nodded. "Peregrine
Beverley, very much at your service—late of Beverley Place, Surrey, now of Nowhere-in-Particular."

"Beverley," I said again. "I have heard
that name before."

"It is highly probable, Mr. Vibart. A fool of
that name—fortunate or unfortunate as you
choose to classify him—lost houses, land, and
money in a single night's play. I am that fool, Sir,
though you have doubtless heard particulars before now?"

"Not a word!" I said.

Mr. Beverley glanced at me with a faint
mingling of pity and surprise.

"My life," I explained, "has been altogether
a studious one, with the not altogether unnat-

ural result that I also am bound for Nowhere-in-Particular, with just eight shillings and sixpence in my pocket."

"And mine, as I tell you," he said, "has been an altogether riotous one. In my career, episodically brief though it was, I have met and talked with all the wits and celebrated men, have drunk good wine, and have worshipped beautiful women, Mr. Vibart."

"And what has it all taught you?" I asked.

"That there are an infernal number of rogues and rascals in the world, for one thing—and that is worth knowing."

"Yes," I replied.

"That, though money can buy anything, from the love of a woman to the death of an enemy it can only be spent once—and that is worth knowing also."

"Yes," I said.

"And that I am the most preposterous ass—and that last, look you, is more valuable than all the others."

Having remarked which, he lay flat on his back again, staring up at the leaves and the calm serenity of the sky beyond, while I filled my negro-head pipe from my paper of tobacco and forthwith began to smoke.

And presently, as I sat alternately watching the blue wreathes of my pipe and the bedraggled figure extended beside me, he suddenly rolled over on his arm, and so lay, watching me.

"On my soul!" he exclaimed at length. "It is positively marvellous."

"What is?" I enquired.

"The resemblance between you and your famous cousin."

"It would appear so," I said, shrugging my shoulders, "though personally I was unaware of this fact up till now."

"Do I understand that you have never seen Sir Maurice Vibart, never seen 'Buck' Vibart?"

"Never!" I replied.

"Nevertheless, the resemblance between you both in face and figure is positively astounding! With the sole exception that he wears hair upon his face, and is of a ruddy complexion, while you are pale and smooth-cheeked as—as a boy . . ."

"Or yourself!" I said.

"Ah—exactly!" he answered, and passed his fingers across his chin tentatively, and fell again to staring lazily up into the sky.

"Do you happen to know anything about that most remarkable species calling themselves 'Bucks' or 'Corinthians'?" he enquired after a while.

"Very well," I said, "and that, only by hearsay."

"Well, up to six months ago, I was one of them, Mr. Vibart, until Fortune wisely decreed it otherwise."

And herewith, lying upon his back, looking up through the quivering green of leaves, he told mad tales of a reckless Prince, of the placid

Brummell, of the "dashing" Vibart, of the brilliant Sheridan, Fox, and Grattan, and of many others whose names are now a byword one way or the other.

He recounted a story of wild prodigality, of drunken midnight orgies, of days and nights over the cards, of wine, women, and horses. But lastly, and very reverently, he spoke of a woman, of her love, and faith, and deathless trust.

"Of course," he ended, "I might have starved very comfortably, and much quicker, in London, but when my time comes, I prefer to do my dying beneath some green hedge, or in the shelter of some friendly rick, with the cool, clean wind upon my face. Besides—she loved the country."

"Then there are some women who can't be bought?" I said, looking at his glistening eyes.

"Mr. Vibart," he said, "so far as I know there are two—the Lady Helen Dunstan and the 'Glorious' Sefton."

"The Lady Sophia Sefton of Cambourne?" I said.

"And—the Lady Helen Dunstan," he repeated.

"Do you know the Lady Sophia Sefton?"

"I have had the honour of dancing with her frequently," he answered.

"And is she so beautiful as they say?"

"She is the handsomest woman in London, one of your black-browed, deep-eyed goddesses, tall and gracious, and most nobly shaped; though,

Sir, for my own part, I prefer less fire and ice—a more ... gentle beauty."

"As, for instance—the Lady Helen Dunstan?" I said.

"Exactly!" Mr. Beverley nodded.

"Referring to the Lady Sophia Sefton," I pursued, "she is a reigning toast, I believe?"

"Gad, yes! Her worshippers are legion and chief amongst them His Royal Highness, and your cousin, Sir Maurice, who has actually had the temerity to enter the field as the Prince's avowed rival—no one but Buck Vibart could be so madly rash!"

"A most fortunate lady!" I said.

"Mr. Vibart!" exclaimed my companion cocking his battered hat and regarding me with a smouldering eye. "Mr. Vibart, I object to your tone; the noble Sefton's virtue is proud, and high, and above even the breath of suspicion."

"And yet my cousin would seem to be no laggard in love, and as to the Prince—his glance is contamination to a woman."

"Sir," returned Mr. Beverley very earnestly, "disabuse your mind of all unworthy suspicions, I beg; your cousin she laughs to scorn, and His Royal Highness she has rebuffed as few women have hitherto dared."

"It would almost seem," I said after a pause, "that from what I have inadvertently learned, my cousin has some dirty work afoot, though exactly what, I cannot imagine."

"My dear Mr. Vibart, your excellent cousin is forever up to something or other, and has escaped the well-merited consequences more than once, owing to his friendship with, and the favour of, his friend . . ."

"George?" I said.

"Exactly!" said my companion, raising himself on his elbow and nodding. "George."

"Have you ever heard mention of Tom Cragg, the Pugilist?" I enquired, blowing a cloud of smoke into the warm air.

"I won ten thousand guineas when he knocked out Ted Jarraway of Swansea." My companion yawned. "A good fighter, but a rogue—like all the rest of 'em—and a creature of your excellent cousin's."

"I guessed as much." I nodded, and forthwith plunged into an account of my meeting with the "craggy one," which seemed to amuse Mr. Beverley mightily, more especially when I related Cragg's mysterious disappearance.

"Oh gad!" cried Beverley, wiping his eyes on the tattered lapel of his coat. "The resemblance served you luckily there; your cousin gave him the thrashing of his life, and poor Tom evidently thought he was in for another. That was the last you saw of him, I'll be bound."

"No, I met him afterwards beneath the gibbet on River Hill, where, among other incomprehensible things, he gave me to understand that

34

he recognised me despite my disguise, assumed, as he supposed, on account of his having kidnapped someone or other and 'laid out' a certain Sir Jasper Trent in Wyeth Street according to my orders, or rather, it would seem, my cousin's orders, the author of which outrage Sir Jasper had evidently found out...."

"The devil!" exclaimed Mr. Beverley as he sat up with a jerk.

"And furthermore," I went on, "he informed me that the Prince himself had given him the word to leave London until the affair had 'blown over.'"

Now while I spoke Mr. Beverley had been regarding me with a very strange expression, his cheeks had gone even paler than before, his eyes seemed to stare through and beyond me, and his hands were tight-clenched at his sides.

"Mr. Beverley," I said, "what ails you?"

For a moment he did not speak, then answered, with the same strange look:

"Sir Jasper Trent—is my cousin, Sir."

My negro-head pipe slipped suddenly and fell into the grass, happily without injury.

"Indeed!" I said.

"Can you not see what this means, Sir?" he went on hurriedly. "Jasper will fight."

"Indeed," I said again, "I fear so."

"Jasper was always a bit of a fish, and with no particular affection for his graceless kinsman, but I am his only relative; and—and he hardly knows one end of a pistol from the other, while your cousin is a dead shot."

"My cousin!" I exclaimed. "Then it was he—to be sure I saw only his back."

"Sir Jasper is unmarried—has no relations but myself," my companion repeated with the same fixed intentness of look. "Can you appreciate what this would mean to me?"

"Rank and fortune and London," I said.

"No, no!" he sprang to his feet, and threw wide his ragged arms with a swift, passionate gesture. "It means Life—and Helen.

"My God!" he went on, speaking almost in a whisper. "I never knew how much I wanted her —how much I had wilfully tossed aside—till now! I never realised the full misery of it all—till now! I could have starved very well in time, and managed it as quietly as most other ruined fools.

"But now—to see the chance of beginning again, of coming back to self-respect and—Helen, my God!"

And suddenly he cast himself upon his face, and so lay tearing up the grass by handfuls. Then, almost as suddenly, he was upon his feet again and had caught up his hat.

"Sir," he said, somewhat shamefacedly, smoothing its ruffled nap with fingers that still quivered, "pray forgive that little ebullition of feeling, it is over—quite over—but your tidings affected me, and I am not quite myself at times."

"Indeed," I said, "you seemed strangely perturbed."

"Mr. Vibart," he said, staring very hard at the battered hat, and turning it round and round, "Mr. Vibart, the devil is surprisingly strong in some of us."

"True," I said.

"My cousin, Sir Jasper, is a bookish fellow, and, as I have said, a fool where anything else is in question. If this meeting is allowed to take place, I feel that he will certainly be killed, and his death would mean a new life—more than life —to me."

"Yes," I said.

"And for a moment, Mr. Vibart, I was tempted to sit down in the ditch again, and let things take their course. The devil, I repeat, is remarkably strong in some of us."

"Then what is your present intention?"

"I am going to London to find Sir Maurice Vibart—to stop this duel."

"Impossible," I said.

"But you see, Sir, it so happens that I am possessed of certain intelligence which might make Sir Maurice's existence in England positively untenable."

"Nevertheless," I said, "it is impossible."

"That remains to be seen, Mr. Vibart," he said, and turned upon his heel.

"One moment," I said, "was not your cousin, Sir Jasper, of the middle height, slim-built, and fair-haired, with a habit of plucking at his lips when at all nervous, or excited?"

"Exactly. You know him, Sir?"

"No," I answered, "but I have seen him, very lately, and I say again, to stop this duel is an impossibility."

"Do you mean . . ." he began, and paused. Now as his eyes met mine the battered hat escaped his fingers, and lay all unheeded.

"Do you mean . . ." he began again, and again stopped.

"Yes," I said, "I mean that you are too late. Sir Jasper was killed at a place called Deepdene Wood, no longer since than today at half-past seven in the morning. It was raining at the time, I remember, but the day grew glorious later."

For a long moment Mr. Beverley stood silent, with bent head, then apparently becoming aware of the hat at his feet, he sent it flying with a sudden kick.

He watched it describe a wide parabola before it disappeared into the ditch, some yards away. Then he walked after it, and returned, brushing it very carefully with his ragged cuff.

"And—you are sure—quite sure, Mr. Vibart?" he enquired, smoothing the broken brim with the greatest solicitude.

"I stood behind a hedge, and watched it done," I said.

"Then—my God—I am Sir Peregrine Beverley! I am Sir Peregrine Beverley, of Burnham

Hall, very much at your service. Jasper—dead! A Knight Baronet of Kent, and Justice of the Peace —how utterly preposterous it all sounds!

"But today I begin life anew, ah yes, a new life, a new life! Today all things are possible again! The fool has learned wisdom and, I hope, become a man.

"But come," he said in a more natural tone, "let us get back to our ditch, and while you tell me the particulars, if you don't object I should much like to try a whiff at that pipe of yours."

So, while I recounted the affair as briefly as I might, he sat puffing at my pipe, and staring away into the distance. But gradually his head sank lower and lower, until his face was quite hidden from me, and for a long moment after I had ended my narration, there was silence.

"Poor Jasper!" he said at last, without raising his head. "Poor old Jasper!"

"I congratulate you, Sir Peregrine," I said.

"And I used to pummel him so, when we were boys together at Eton—poor old Jasper!"

And presently he handed me my pipe and rose.

"Mr. Vibart," he said, "had I not met with you, it is—rather more than probable—that I— should never have seen another dawn; so if—if ever I can be of use to you, pray honour me so far, you can always hear of me at Burnham Hall, Pembry.

"Good-bye, Mr. Vibart, I am going to her—in all my rags—for I am a man again."

So I bade him good-bye, and, sitting in the ditch, watched him stride away to his new life.

Presently, reaching the brow of the hill (there are hills everywhere in the South country), I saw him turn to flourish the battered hat before he disappeared from my sight.

*   *   *

That night I took lodging in a wayside tavern. In the early hours I was suddenly awakened by a sound outside my room, and, unable to sleep again, I lay for a while in the darkness.

Then I became conscious of yet another sound, indescribably desolate: the low, repressed sound of a woman sobbing.

I rose, and looking down into the lane, found it deserted. I noticed that the casement next to mine had been opened wide, and it was from there, as it seemed, that the weeping proceeded.

After some hesitation, I knocked softly upon the wall, at which the weeping was checked abruptly, save for an occasional sob, whereupon I presently rapped again.

At this, after a moment or so, I saw a very small, white hand appear at the neighbouring window, and the next moment I was looking into a lovely, flushed face framed in bright hair, with eyes woefully swelled by tears—but a glance showed me that she was young, and of a rare and gentle beauty.

Before I could speak she laid her finger upon her lip with a warning gesture.

"Help me—oh, help me!" she whispered hurriedly. "They have locked me in here, and I dare not go to bed, and . . . and . . . oh, what shall I do?"

"Locked you in?" I exclaimed.

"Oh, what shall I do?" she sobbed. "I tell you I am afraid of him . . . his hateful, wicked eyes!"

Here a tremor seemed to shake her, and she covered her face with her hands.

"Tonight, when I found the key gone from the door and remembered his look as he bade me good-night, I thought I should have died.

"I waited here, close beside the window . . . listening, listening. Once I thought I heard a step outside my door, and opened the casement to throw myself out. . . . He shall not find me here when he comes."

All this she had imparted to me in broken whispers, and with her face still hidden, but at my words she peeped at me through her fingers.

"You must run away," I said.

"But the door is locked."

"There remains the window."

"The window!" she repeated, trembling.

"You would find it easy enough with my help."

"Quick, then!" she exclaimed, and held out her hand.

"Wait," I said, and turned back into my room.

Hereupon, having locked the door, I got into my boots, slipped on my coat and knapsack, threw my blackthorn staff out the window (where I was sure of finding it), and last of all climbed out after it.

The porch I have mentioned, upon which I now stood, sloped steeply down upon two sides, so that I had no little difficulty in maintaining my foothold; on the other hand, it was no great distance from the ground, and I thought that it would be an easy enough descent.

At this moment the lady reappeared at the lattice.

"What is it?" I whispered, struck by the terror in her face.

"Quick!" she cried, forgetting all prudence in her fear. "Quick ... they are coming ... I hear someone upon the stair. Oh, you are too late!"

Sinking upon her knees, she covered her face with her hands.

Without more ado, I swung myself up and clambered over the sill into the room beside her.

I was looking round for something that might serve me for a weapon when my eye encountered a tall oak press, a heavy, cumbersome affair, but, save the bed, the only furniture the room possessed.

Setting my shoulder to it, therefore, I began to urge it towards the door.

But it was soon apparent that I could not get there in time, for the creeping footstep was already close outside, and the next moment a key was softly inserted in the lock.

"Quick! Hide yourself!" I whispered over my shoulder.

Stepping back from the door to give myself room, I clenched my fists. There was a faint creak as the key turned, the door was opened cautiously, and a man's dim figure loomed upon the threshold.

He had advanced two or three paces on tiptoe before he discovered my presence, for the room was in shadow, and I heard his breath catch, suddenly, and hiss between his teeth; then, without a word, he sprang at me.

But as he came, I leapt aside, and my fist took him full and squarely beneath the ear. He pitched sideways, and falling heavily, rolled over upon his back, and lay still.

I dragged him out into the passage, whipped the key from the lock, transferred it to the inside, and closing the door locked it.

Waiting for no more, I scrambled back through the casement and reached up my hand to the lady.

"Come," I said, and she was beside me upon the roof of the porch, clinging to my arm.

Our farther descent to the ground proved much more difficult than I had supposed, but, though I could feel her trembling, my companion obeyed my whispered instructions, and we were soon standing in the lane before the house, safe and sound except for a few rents to our garments.

"What is it?" she whispered, seeing me searching about in the grass.

"My staff," I said, "a faithful friend, I would not lose it."

"But they will be here in a minute ... we shall be seen."

"I cannot lose my staff," I said.

"Oh, hurry! Hurry!" she cried, wringing her hands.

And in a little while, having found my staff, we turned our backs upon the tavern and began to run up the lane, side by side.

As we went came the slam of a door behind us, a sudden clamour of voices, followed, a moment later, by the sharp report of a pistol, and in that same fraction of time, I stumbled over some unseen obstacle, and my hat was whisked from my head.

"Are you hurt?" my companion asked, panting.

"No," I said, "but it was a very excellent shot nevertheless!" For, as I picked up my hat, I saw a small round hole midway between crown and brim.

We had traversed some half-mile, when my ears warned me that our pursuers were gaining upon us.

I was inwardly congratulating myself that I had stopped to find my staff, when I found that my companion was no longer at my side.

As I paused, irresolute, her voice reached me from the shadow of the hedge.

"This way," she said, panting.

"Where?" I said.

"Here!" And, as she spoke, her hand slipped into mine.

She led me through a small gate and into a broad, open meadow beyond. But to attempt crossing this would be little short of madness, for we could not go a yard without being seen.

"No, no," she returned, her breath still labouring. "Wait . . . wait till they are past."

So, hand in hand, we stood there in the shadow, screened very effectively from the lane by the thick hedge, while the rush of our pursuer's feet drew nearer and nearer, until we could hear a voice that panted out curses upon the dark lane, ourselves, and everything concerned.

At this my companion seemed to fall into a shivering fit, her clasp tightened upon my hand, and she drew closer to me.

Thus we remained until voices and footsteps had grown faint with distance, but even then I could feel that she was trembling still.

Suddenly she drew her fingers from mine and covered her face with her hands.

"Oh, that man!" she exclaimed in a whisper.

"I didn't quite realise till now . . . what I have escaped. Oh, that beast!"

"Sir Harry Mortiner?" I said.

"You know him?" she cried.

"Heaven forbid!" I answered. "But I have seen him once before at the Chequers Inn at Tonbridge, and I never forget names or faces—especially such as his."

"How I hate him!" she whispered.

"An unpleasant animal, to be sure," I said. "But come, it is wiser to get as far from here as possible, for they will doubtless be returning soon."

So we started off again, running in the shadow of the hedge. We had thus doubled back upon our pursuers, and leaving the tavern upon our left, soon gained the kindly shadow of those woods through which I had passed in the early evening.

Borne to us upon the gentle wind was the haunting perfume of hidden flowers, and the sinking moon sent long shafts of silvery light to pierce the leafy gloom and make the shadows more mysterious.

The path we followed was very narrow, so that sometimes my companion's knee touched mine, or her long, silken hair brushed my brow or cheek, as I stooped to lift some trailing branch that barred her way, or open a path for her through the leaves.

So we journeyed on through the mysteries of the woods together.

At last coming to a broad, grassy glade, the lady paused and, standing in the full radiance of the dying moon, looked up at me with a smile on her red lips.

"They can never find us now!" she said.

"No, they can never find us now," I repeated.

"And . . . oh, Sir! I can never, never thank you," she began.

"Don't," I said, not looking at her; "don't thank me till—we are out of the wood."

"I think," she went on slowly, "that you . . . can guess from . . . from what you saved me, and can understand something of my gratitude, for I can never express it all."

"Indeed," I said, "indeed you overestimate my service."

"You risked your life for me, Sir," she said, her eyes glistening. "Surely my thanks are due to you for that? And I do thank you . . . from my heart!"

And with a swift, impulsive gesture, she stretched out her hands to me.

For a brief moment I hesitated, then seized them and drew her close. But even as I stooped above her, she repulsed me desperately; her loosened hair brushed my eyes and lips—blinded, maddened me; my hat fell off, and all at once her struggles ceased.

"Sir Maurice Vibart!" she said, panting.

I saw a hopeless terror in her face.

My arms tightened about her, then I loosed her suddenly, and turning, smote my clenched fist against a tree; which done, I stooped and picked up my hat and blackthorn staff.

"Madam," I said, looking down upon my bleeding knuckles, "I am not Sir Maurice Vibart. It seems my fate to be mistaken for him wherever I go. My name is Peter, plain and unvarnished, and I am very humbly your servant.

"Come," I said, extending my hand to the trembling girl, "let us go out of these dismal woods."

For a space she hesitated, looking up at me beneath her lashes, then reached out and laid her fingers in mind, and we turned away.

"It is strange," I said, after we had gone some little distance, "very strange that you should only have discovered his resemblance here, and now, for surely you saw my face plainly enough at the Inn."

"No; you see, I hardly looked at you."

"And now that you do look at me, am I so very much like Sir Maurice?"

"Not now," she answered, shaking her head, "for though you are of his height, and though your features are much the same as his, your expression is different."

So we went upon our way, not pausing until we had left the dark woods behind us.

Then I looked from the beauty of the sweet, pure earth to the beauty of she who stood beside me, and I saw that her glance rested upon the broken knuckles of my right hand.

Meeting my eyes, her own drooped, and a flush crept into her cheeks.

*　　*　　*

The moon was fast sinking below the tree-tops to our left by the time we reached a road, or rather cart-track, that wound away up a hill.

Faint and far a church clock slowly chimed the hour of three, the solemn notes coming sweet and silvery with distance.

"What chimes are those?" I enquired.

"Cranbrook Church."

"Is it far to Cranbrook?"

"One mile this way, but two by the road yonder."

"You seem very well acquainted with these parts," I said.

"I have lived here all my life . . . those are the Cambourne Woods over there. . . ."

"Cambourne Woods!" I said.

"Part of the Sefton estates," she continued; "Cambourne village lies to the right, beyond."

"The Lady Sophia Sefton of Cambourne!" I said thoughtfully.

"My dearest friend." My companion nodded.

"They say she is very handsome," I said.

"Then they speak the truth, Sir."

"She has been described to me," I went on, "as a peach, a goddess, and a plum; which should you consider the most proper term?"

My companion shot an arch glance at me from the corners of her eyes, and I saw a dimple come and go, beside the curve of her mouth.

"Goddess, to be sure," she said; "peaches have such rough skins, and plums are apt to be sticky."

"And goddesses," I added, "were all very well upon Olympus, but in this matter-of-fact age must be sadly out of place. Speaking for myself . . ."

"Have you ever seen this particular goddess?" enquired my companion.

"Never."

"Then wait until you have, Sir."

The moon was down now, yet the summer sky was wonderfully luminous and in the east I almost fancied I could detect the first faint gleam of day.

After we had traversed some distance in silence, my companion suddenly spoke, but without looking at me.

"You have never once asked who I am," she said, almost reproachfully I thought, "nor how I came to be shut up in such a place . . . with such a man."

"Why, as to that," I answered, "I make it a general rule to avoid awkward subjects when I

can, and never to ask questions that will be difficult to answer."

"I should find not the least difficulty in answering either," she said.

"Besides," I continued, "it is no affair of
mine, after all."

"Oh!" she said, turning away from me; and
then, very slowly; "no, I suppose not."

"Certainly not," I added; "how should it be?"

"How indeed!" she said over her shoulder.
And then I saw that she was angry, and wondered.

"And yet," I went on, after a lapse of silence,
"I think I could have answered both questions
the moment I saw you at your casement."

"Oh!" she said, this time in a tone of surprise, and her anger was all gone again, for I saw
that she was smiling; and again I wondered.

"Yes." I nodded.

"Then," she said, seeing that I was silent,
"whom do you suppose me?"

"You are, to the best of my belief, the Lady
Helen Dunstan."

My companion stood still, and regarded me
for a moment in wide-eyed astonishment.

"And how, Sir, pray, did you learn all this?"
she demanded, with the dimple once more peeping at me slyly from the corner of her pretty
mouth.

"By the simple method of adding two and

two together," I answered; "moreover, no longer since than yesterday I broke bread with a certain Mr. Beverley ..."

I heard her breath come in a sudden gasp, and the next moment she was peering up into my face while her hands beat upon my breast with soft, quick little taps.

"Beverley?" she whispered. "Beverley ... no ... no ... why, they told me ... Sir Harry told me that Peregrine lay dying ... at Tonbridge."

"Then Sir Harry Mortimer lied to you," I said, "for no longer ago than yesterday afternoon I sat in a ditch eating bread and cheese with a Mr. Peregrine Beverley."

"Oh ... are you sure ... are you sure?"

"Quite sure. And, as we ate, he told me many things, and among them, of a life of wasted opportunities."

"My poor Perry!" she murmured.

"He spoke also of his love for a very beautiful and good woman, and its hopelessness."

"My dear, dear Perry!" she said again. "And is he well? Quite ... quite well?"

"He is," I said.

"Thank God!" she whispered. "Tell me," she went on, "is he so very, very poor ... is he much altered? I have not seen him for a whole, long year."

"Why, a year is apt to change a man," I answered. "Adversity is a hard school, but sometimes a very good one."

"Were he changed, no matter how ... were he a beggar upon the roads, I should love him ... always!" she said, speaking in that soft, caressing voice which only the best of women possess.

"Yes, I had guessed as much," I said, and found myself sighing.

"A year is a long, long time, and we were to have been married this month, but my father quarrelled with him, and forbade him the house, so poor Perry went back to London.

"Then we heard he was ruined, and I almost died with grief ... you see, his very poverty only made me love him the more. Yesterday ... that man ..."

"Sir Harry Mortimer?" I said.

"Yes. He was a friend of whom I had often heard Perry speak, and he told me that my Perry lay at Tonbridge dying, and begged to see me before the end. He offered to escort me to him, assuring me that I could reach home again long before dusk.

"My father, who I knew would never permit me to go, was absent, and so ... I ran away.

"Sir Harry had a carriage waiting, but almost as soon as the door was closed upon us, and we had started, I began to be afraid of him and ... and ..."

"Sir Harry, as I said before, is an unpleasant animal." I nodded.

"Thank Heaven, we had not gone very far

before the chaise broke down! And . . . the rest you know."

The footpath we had been following now led over a stile into a narrow lane or byway. Very soon we came to a high stone wall wherein was set a small wicket.

Through this she led me, and we entered a broad park where there was an avenue of fine old trees, beyond which I saw the gables of a house, for the stars had long since paled to the dawn, and there was a glory in the east.

"Your father will be rejoiced to have you safely back again," I said.

"Yes," she nodded, "but he will be very angry."

And hereupon she stopped and began to pull and twist and pat her shining hair with dexterous white fingers.

She turned, and truly, I thought, the face peeping out from its clustered curls was even more lovely and bewitching than before.

As we approached the house, I saw that the smooth gravel was much cut up as though by the coming and going of many wheels, and horses, and also that one of the windows still shone with a bright light, and it was towards this window that my companion led me.

Now, looking through into the room beyond, I beheld an old man who sat bowed down at a table, with his white head pillowed upon his arms, sitting so very still that he might have been asleep but for the fierce grip of his twitching hands.

Now upon the table, at no great distance from him, lay a hat—a very ill-used, battered-looking object which I thought I recognised; wherefore, looking about, I presently saw its owner leaning against the mantel.

He was powdered with dust from head to foot, and his worn garments looked more ragged than ever.

As he stood there, in the droop of his head and the listless set of his shoulders there was an air of the most utter dejection and hopelessness, while upon his thin cheek I saw the glisten of a great, solitary tear. But as I looked, the window was burst suddenly open.

"Perry!"

Love, surprise, joy, pity, all were summed up in that one short word, yet deeper than all was love. And, at that cry, the white head was raised, raised in time to see a vision of loveliness caught up in two ragged arms.

"Father!"

And now the three heads, the white, the golden, and the black, were drawn together, drawn, and held close in an embrace that was indeed reunion.

Then, seeing my presence had become wholly unnecessary, I turned away, and was soon, once more, deep among the trees. Yet, as I went, I suddenly heard voices that called upon my name, but I kept on, and in due season came out upon the broad highway.

And in a little, as I went, very full of thought, the sun rose up. So I walked along through a world all glorious with morning.

Chapter
Three

The sun was high when, some days later, I came to a place where the ways divided. While I stood hesitating over which road to take, I heard the cool splash and murmur of a brook nearby.

On I went, climbing down as best I could, until I found myself in a sort of green basin, very cool after the heat and glare of the road, for the high, tree-clad sides afforded much shade.

So I walked on beside the brook, watching the fish that looked like darting shadows on the bottom, until, chancing to raise my eyes, I stopped.

There, screened by leaves, shut in among the green, stood a small cottage or hut. My second glance showed it to be tenantless, for the thatch was partly gone, the windows were broken, and the door had long since fallen from its hinges.

Yet, despite its forlornness and desolation,

there was something in the air of the place that drew me strangely.

'A man might do worse than live here,' I thought. And with this in mind I walked on towards the village of Sissinghurst, where I found the Bull. I had one penny left.

This was a charming Inn, with wooden seats positioned outside, upon which were assembled several of what I took to be the inhabitants of the village.

I struck up a conversation with some of them and soon chanced to learn that the village blacksmith was in need of an assistant.

Having already decided to stay awhile in this pleasant spot, I made up my mind to seek the fellow out, and as soon as my ale was finished I set out for the forge.

"Black George," as the smith was known in the village, viewed me at first with suspicion but at last agreed to take me in for a period, and I set to at once to learn the noble art of the smith.

Over the next few weeks, Black George and I worked together, and I began to feel a friendship for this big, silent man, whose nickname referred more to his temper than to his colouring, which was ruddy gold.

I also observed particularly the way his face would light up whenever a certain young lady would come by.

This was Prue, granddaughter of an old man

generally known as "the Ancient," who would fetch our supper baskets of an evening.

One evening Prue arrived with her basket as usual.

Very fair and sweet she looked, lithe and vigorous, and straight as a young poplar, with her shining black hair curling into little tight rings about her ears, and with great, shy eyes, and a red, red mouth.

Surely a man might seek very far before he found such another maid as this brown-cheeked, black-eyed village beauty.

"Good-evening, Mr. Peter!" she said, dropping me a curtsey with a grace that could not have been surpassed by any Duchess in the land.

But as for poor George, she did not even notice him; neither did he raise his curly head nor glance towards her.

"You come just when you are most needed, Prudence," I said, relieving her of the heavy basket, "for we are two hungry men."

"Three!" broke in the Ancient. "So hungry as a lion, I am!"

"Three hungry men, Prudence, who have been listening for your step this half-hour and more."

"For the sake of my basket?" Prudence asked shyly.

"No," I replied, shaking my head. "Basket or

no basket, you are equally welcome, Prudence. Isn't that so, George?"

But George only mumbled in his beard, and the Ancient and I now set to work, putting up an extemporised table.

As for George, he stood staring down moodily into the glowing embers of the forge.

Having put up the table, I crossed to where Prudence was busy unpacking her basket.

"Prudence," I said, "are you still at odds with George?"

Prudence nodded.

"But," I continued, "he is such a splendid fellow! That outburst the other day was quite natural, under the circumstances—surely you can forgive him, Prudence."

" 'Tis more than that, Mr. Peter." Prue sighed. " 'Tis his drinkin'; six months ago he promised me never to touch another drop—and he broke his word."

"But surely good ale, in moderation, will harm no one, on the contrary . . ."

"But Jarge isn't like other men, Mr. Peter!"

"No, he is much bigger, and stronger!" I said. "And I never saw a handsomer fellow."

"Yes," the girl nodded, "so strong as a giant, an' so weak as a little child!"

So we presently sat down, all three of us, while Prudence carved, and supplied our wants, as only Prudence could. Afterwards, as we sat smoking our pipes, she packed her basket and left us alone.

"She'll make some man a fine wife someday!" exclaimed the Ancient, blowing out a cloud of smoke.

"You speak my very thought, Ancient," I said, "she will indeed. What do you think, George?"

But George's answer was to choke suddenly in a fit of coughing.

"Smoke go t' wrong way, Jarge?" enquired the Ancient, fixing him with his bright eye.

"Ay." George nodded.

"Ha!" said the old man; and we smoked for a time in silence.

"'andsome as a picture she be!" the Ancient said suddenly.

"She is fairer than any picture," I replied impulsively, "and what is better still, her nature is as sweet and beautiful as her face!"

"How do you know that?" George said, turning sharply on me.

"My eyes and ears tell me so, as yours surely must have done long ago," I answered.

"You do not think as she be a pretty lass, then, Peter?" enquired the Ancient.

"I think," I said, "that she is the prettiest lass I ever saw—don't you think so, George?"

But again George's only answer was to choke.

"Smoke again, Jarge?" enquired the Ancient.

"Ay." said George, as before.

"Talking about Prue," said the Ancient, glancing at each of us in turn, "there was some folks that used to think she was sweet on Jarge there, but I, being 'er lawful grandfather, knew different—didn't I, Jarge?"

"Ay." The smith nodded.

"Many's the time I've said to you, sitting in this very corner, 'Jarge,' I've said, 'mark my words, Jarge—if ever my Prue does marry someone—which she will—that someone won't be you.' Those were my very words, weren't they, Jarge?"

"Your very words, Gaffer." George nodded.

"Well then," continued the old man, "'ere's what I was coming to—Prue's fallen in love with someone at last."

Black George's pipe shivered to fragments on the floor, and as he leaned forward I saw that his great hands were tightly clenched.

"What do you mean?" he said in a strangled voice.

"I mean what I says."

"How do you know?"

"Aren't I the lass's grandfather?"

"Are you sure—quite sure?"

"Yes, certain sure—twice this week and once the week before she forgot to put any salt in the soup, and that speaks volumes, Jarge, volumes!"

Here, having replaced his snuff-box, the Ancient put on his hat, nodded, and hobbled away.

As for Black George, he sat there, staring blindly before him long after the tapping of the Ancient's stick had died away.

Nor did he hear me when I spoke, so I laid my hand upon his shoulder.

"Come, George," I said, "another hour and the work will be finished."

He started, and, drawing from my hand, looked up at me strangely.

"No, Peter," he mumbled, "I can't work any more tonight," and as he spoke he rose to his feet.

"What—are you going?" I said, as he crossed to the door.

"Yes, I'm going."

Now, as he went towards his cottage, I saw him reel, and stagger, like a drunken man.

*   *   *

"George," I said, on a certain Saturday morning, as I washed the grime from my face and hands, "are you going to the Fair this afternoon?"

"No, Peter, I aren't."

"But Prudence is going."

"Supposing she is going to the Fair, what's that to me? I don't care where she comes, no, nor where she goes, neither!"

"Has it ever struck you that Prudence is an uncommonly handsome girl?"

"To be sure it has—I'm not blind."

"And other men have seen it too."

"Well, Peter?"

"And maybe someone even told her so? And —maybe asked her to marry him, George?"

This time he was silent so long that I had tied my neckerchief and drawn on my coat before he spoke, very heavily and slowly, and without looking at me.

"Why then, Peter, let him. I've told you before, I don't care where she comes nor where she goes; she isn't anything to me any more, nor I to her. And now let's talk of something else."

"Willingly. There's to be boxing, singlestick, and wrestling at the Fair, I understand. And they tell me there is a famous wrestler coming all the way from Cornwall to wrestle the best man for ten guineas."

"Yes, there is."

"They were saying that you were a mighty wrestler, George, that you were the only man in these parts who could stand up to this Cornishman."

"No, Peter."

"And why not?"

"Because I haven't got the mind to—because I am never going to wrestle again, Peter, so there's an end to it."

Yet, in the doorway I paused and looked back.

"George. Won't you come—for friendship's sake?"

Black George picked up his coat, looked at it, and put it down again.

"No, Peter!"

*　　*　　*

Above the merry hubbub rose the blare of trumpets, the braying of horns, and the crash and rattle of drums—in a word, I was in the middle of an English Country Fair.

There were circuses and shows of all kinds, where one could see strange beasts and the usual Fat Women and Skeleton Men.

Though I looked all round the Fair, I saw nothing of the Ancient. As evening was falling, I turned round to make my way home, when I came to a part of the Fair where drinking booths had been set up, and where they were preparing to roast a whole ox, as is the immemorial custom.

Two or three times I was rudely jostled as I made my way along, so that my temper was already rising when, turning aside to avoid all this, I came upon two fellows, well-to-do farmers by the look of them, who held a struggling girl between them.

I reached out a hand to each of them, and, gripping them firmly by their collars, brought their two heads together with a resounding crack —and then I saw that the girl was Prudence.

The next moment we were running, hand in hand, with the two fellows roaring in pursuit.

But Prudence was so wonderfully swift and light-footed, doubling and turning among carts, tents, and booths, that we had outstripped our pursuers and lost them completely.

In spite of this, Prudence still kept running, till, catching her foot in some obstacle, she tripped, and would have fallen but for my arm.

And looking down into her flushed face, glowing through the sweet disorder of her glossy curls, I could not help thinking how lovely she was. But, as I watched, the colour fled from her cheeks, her eyes dilated, and she moved away from me.

Turning hastily, I saw that we were standing close by a small, dirty, and disreputable-looking tent, the canvas of which had been slit with a knife—and my movement had been quick enough to enable me to see a face vanish through the canvas.

And fleeting though the glimpse had been, in the baleful glare of his eyes and the set of the great jaw I had seen—Death.

And after we had walked on awhile together, looking at Prue, I noticed that she trembled.

"Oh, Mr. Peter," she whispered, glancing back over her shoulder, "did you see?"

"Yes, Prudence, I saw."

And, speaking, I also glanced back towards the villainous little tent, and though the face appeared no more, I was aware, nevertheless, of a sudden misgiving that was almost like a fore-boding of evil to come.

For in those features, disfigured though they were with black rage and passion, I had recognised the face of Black George.

Chapter
Four

One evening I sat dozing by the fire in my cottage while a storm raged outside. Suddenly I was awakened from a very vivid dream in which I had seemed to hear a voice crying the name "Charmian!"

Shivering, I was reaching for my tobacco to refill my pipe, when I heard the cry again, nearer this time.

Then, all at once, the door of the cottage burst open with a crash, and immediately the quiet room was full of rioting wind. And borne on this wind, like some spirit of the storm, was a woman with flying draperies and long, streaming hair, who forced the door shut and leaned there, panting.

She was tall and nobly shaped, for her wet gown clung, disclosing the sinuous lines of her waist and the bold, full curves of hip and thigh.

Her dress, too, had been wrenched and torn at the neck, and through the shadow of her fallen hair I caught the ivory gleam of her shoulder, and the heave and tumult of her bosom.

The woman crouched back against the wall, with her eyes towards the door, and always her right hand was hidden in the folds of her petticoat. So we remained, she watching the door, and I, her.

"Charmian!"

The voice was very near now; and, almost immediately after, a heavy fist pounded upon the door.

"Oh, Charmian, you're there, I know you are. I swore you should never escape me, and you shan't—by God!"

A hand fumbled upon the latch, the door swung open, and a man entered. As he did so, I leapt forward and caught the woman's wrist.

There was a blinding flash, a loud report, and a bullet buried itself somewhere in the rafters overhead. With a strange, repressed cry, she turned upon me so fiercely that I fell back before her.

The newcomer, meanwhile, had closed the door, latching it very carefully; and now, standing before it, he folded his arms, staring at her with bent head.

He was a very tall man, with a rain-sodden, bell-crowned hat crushed low upon his brows, and wrapped in a long, many-caped overcoat, the skirts of which were mud-splattered and torn.

All at once he laughed, very softly and musically.

"So, you would have killed me, would you, Charmian—shot me—like a dog? So you thought you had lost me, did you, when you gave me the slip a while ago? Lose me? Escape me? Why, I tell you, I would search for you day and night, hunt the world over until I found you, Charmian —until I found you!"

The woman neither moved nor uttered a word; only her breath came thick and fast, and her eyes gleamed in the shadow of her hair.

With every passing minute I was becoming more curious to see this man's face, hidden as it was in the shadow of his dripping hat-brim. Yet the fire had burned low.

"You always were a spitfire, weren't you, Charmian?" he went on in the same gentle voice. "Hot and fierce and proud—the flame beneath the ice—I knew that, and loved you the better for it. And so I determined to win you, Charmian, to win you whether you liked it or not. You are so strong, so tall, and glorious, Charmian!"

He drew a step nearer to her.

"And tonight you would have killed me, Charmian—shot me like a dog! You have flouted, coquetted, scorned, and mocked me for three years, and tonight you would have killed me—and I would not have it otherwise, for sure-

ly you can see that this of itself must make your
final surrender—even sweeter."

With a gesture utterly at variance with his
voice, so sudden, fierce, and passionate was it, he
sprang towards her with outstretched arms.

But, quick as he was, she eluded him, and
before he could reach her I stepped between
them.

"Sir," I said, "a word with you."

"Out of my way, bumpkin!" he retorted; and,
brushing me aside, he went after her.

I caught him by his coat, but with a dexterous twist he had left it in my grasp.

Yet the check enabled her to slip through the
door of the other room, and before he could reach
it I stood upon the threshold.

"There are two hundred guineas, bumpkin,
maybe more—pick them up and go!" And, turning, he flung open the door.

Obediently I stooped, and, taking up the
purse, rolled it in the coat which I still held,
and tossed both out of the cottage.

"Sir," I said, "be so very obliging as to follow
your property."

Then suddenly hands were upon my throat,
and I could feel his hot panting breath on my
face. Desperately I strove to break his hold, only
the fingers tightened and tightened.

I beat him with my fists and tore at his
wrists, but he gripped my throat even tighter.

Now we were outside, rolling on the sodden grass, and then we were up, stumbling and slipping, but still the gripping fingers sank deeper, choking the strength and life out of me.

Then we tottered, swayed helplessly, and plunged down together.

But, as we fell, the deadly, gripping fingers slackened for a moment, and in that moment I had broken free, and, rolling clear, stumbled to my feet.

"Where are you?" I said at last.

Receiving no answer, I advanced cautiously (for it was, as I have said, black dark), and so, presently, touched something with my foot.

Hastily I tore open his waistcoat and shirt and pressed my hand above his heart. In that one instant I lived an age of harrowing suspense, then breathed a sigh of relief, and, rising, took him under the arms and began to half-drag, half-carry him towards the cottage.

I had pulled him only about a dozen yards or so when I thought I heard a faint "Hallo," and looking round saw a twinkling light growing brighter each moment. Setting down my burden, I shouted:

"This way!"

"Be that you, Sir?"

"This way!" I called again. "This way!"

As he came up I made him out to be a postillion by his dress, and he carried the lanthorn of a chaise.

"Why—Sir!" he began, looking me up and down by the light of his lanthorn, "strike me lucky if I'd have known you! You looks as if—oh, Lord!"

"What is it?" I asked.

The postillion's answer was to lower his lanthorn towards the face of the man lying on the ground between us, and point.

Now, looking where he pointed, I started suddenly backwards, and shivered, with a strange stirring of the flesh.

For I saw a pale face with a streak of blood upon the cheek; a face framed in lank hair, thick and black—a pale, aquiline face, with a prominent nose, and long, cleft chin. A face with features just like my own.

So, as I stood looking down upon this face, my breath caught and my flesh crept, for indeed, I might have been looking into a mirror—the face was the face of myself.

"Where is your chaise?" I asked at length.

"Up in the lane, somewhere over yonder," he answered, with a vague jerk of his thumb over his shoulder.

"Then, if you will take this gentleman's heels, we can carry him easily between us—it's no great distance."

We presently stumbled upon a chaise and horses, in which we deposited our limp burden as comfortably as we could; and there I tried to tie up the gash in his brow.

"It would be a fine thing," the postillion

said moodily, as I closed the chaise door, "it would be a nice thing if he was to go and die."

"By the look of him," I said, "he will be swearing your head off in the next ten minutes or so."

Without another word, the postillion set the lanthorn back in its socket and swung himself into the saddle.

"Your best course would be to make for Tonbridge, bearing to the right when you strike the high roads."

"Ah!" exclaimed the postillion with a slow nod, and drawing out the word unduly. "What about my second passenger? I started with two and here's just one. Where about Number Two— what about her?"

"Her!" I repeated.

"Her as was with him—Number One—her what was quarrelling with him all the way from London—her as run away from him into the wood. What about Number Two—her?"

"Why, to be sure, I had forgotten her!"

"Forgotten!" repeated the postillion. "Oh, Lord, yes!"

And with a knowing wink he cracked his whip and the horses plunged forward.

Almost immediately, it seemed, horses, chaise, and postillion had lurched into the black murk of the night, and vanished.

Considering everything that had happened

in the last half-hour or so, it was not very surprising, I think, that I should have forgotten this woman Charmian.

Women were to me practically an unknown quantity as yet, and so it was with no little trepidation that I started out for the cottage and this truly Amazonian Charmian, unless she had disappeared as suddenly as she had come (which I found myself devoutly hoping).

It seemed I travelled miles before I felt the latch beneath my fingers, and fumblingly opened the door, stumbled in, and closed it after me.

There was a mist before my eyes, yet I was conscious that the girl had leapt up on my entrance, and now stood confronting me across the table.

"You!" she said, in a low, repressed voice. "You?"

I saw the glitter of steel in her hand.

"Keep back! Keep back . . . I warn you!"

But I only leaned there against the door. And as I stood there, hanging my head and not answering her, she stamped her foot suddenly, and laughed a short, fierce laugh.

"So . . . he has hurt you! Oh, I am glad! I might have run away . . . but you see . . . I was prepared for you."

And she held up the knife.

"The country bumpkin has done his work well. I shall not need this after all . . . see!"

And she flung the knife upon the table.

"Yes, it is better there," I said, "and I think Madam is mistaken."

"Mistaken?" she cried, with a sudden catch in her voice. "What . . . what do you mean?"

"That I am—the bumpkin!" I said.

Now as I spoke a black mist enveloped everything; my knees loosened suddenly, and, stumbling forward, I sank into a chair.

"I am—very—tired!" I sighed, and so, as it seemed, fell asleep.

* * *

She was on her knees beside me, bathing my battered face, talking all the while in a soft voice that I thought wonderfully sweet to hear.

"Poor boy!" she was saying, over and over again. "Poor boy!"

After she had said it perhaps a dozen times, I opened my eyes and looked at her.

A wonderful face—low-browed, deep-eyed, full-lipped. The eyes were dark and swiftly changeful, and there was a subtle witchery in the slanting shadow of their lashes.

"Poor boy!" she said. "Poor boy!"

And, when I would have retorted, she stopped me with the sponge.

"Your mouth is cut, and there is a great gash in your brow."

"But the water feels delicious!"

"And your throat is all scratched and swollen!"

"But your hands are very gentle and soothing!"

"I don't hurt you, then?"

"On the contrary, the—the pain is very trifling, thank you."

"Yet you fainted a little while ago."

"Then it was very foolish of me."

"Poor . . . " she hesitated; and looking up at her through the trickling water, I saw that she was smiling, "fellow!"

Her lips were very sweet and her eyes very soft and tender—for an Amazon.

When she had washed the blood from my face, she went to fetch clean water from where I kept it in a bucket in the corner.

Now, at my elbow, upon the table, lay the knife, a heavy, clumsy contrivance, which I had bought to use in my carpentry, and I mechanically picked it up. As I did so the light gleamed evilly upon its long blade.

"Put it down!" she commanded. "Put it away . . . it is a hateful thing!"

"For a woman's hand," I added, "so hideously unfeminine!"

"Some men are so hatefully, hideously masculine!" she retorted, her lip curling. "I expected . . . him . . . and you are terribly like him."

"I may have the same colour eyes, and hair, and be something of the same build. . . ."

"Yes, it was your build, and the colour of your eyes and hair, that . . . startled me."

"But after all, the similarity is only skin-deep, and goes no farther."

"No," she answered, kneeling beside me again.

"You do not fear me any longer?"

"No."

"In spite of my eyes and hair?"

"In spite of your eyes and hair . . . You see, a woman knows instinctively whom she must fear and whom not to fear."

"And yet, I am very like him, you said so yourself!"

"Him! I had forgotten all about him. Where is he . . . what has become of him?" And she glanced apprehensively towards the door.

"Halfway to Tonbridge—or should be by now."

"Was he . . . badly hurt?"

"Only stunned."

She was still kneeling beside my chair, but now she sat back, and turned to stare into the fire.

I noticed how full and round and white her arms were, for her sleeves were rolled high, and that the hand which still held the sponge was also very white, with long, slender fingers.

Presently, with a sudden gesture, she raised her head and looked at me again—a long, searching look.

"Who are you?" she asked suddenly.

"Peter Smith. I am a blacksmith."

"Peter ... Smith!" she repeated, hesitating at the surname exactly as I had done. "Peter ... Smith! And mine is Charmian. Charmian ... Brown."

Here again was a pause between the two names.

I then started towelling myself vigorously, so much so, that, forgetting the cut in my brow, I made it bleed faster than ever.

"Oh, you are very clumsy!" she cried. Springing up, and snatching the towel from me, she began to staunch the blood with it. "If you will sit down, I will bind it up for you. Is there anything I can use as a bandage?"

"There is the towel!"

"Ridiculous!" she said, and proceeded to draw a handkerchief from the bosom of her dress; and, having folded it with great care, she moistened it in the bowl, then tied it about my temples.

Now, to do this she had to pass her arms about my neck, and this brought her so near that I could feel her breath upon my lips, and there stole to me out of her hair, or out of her bosom, a perfume so very sweet that it was like the fragrance of violets.

"There ... that is more comfortable, isn't it?" she enquired.

With the words, she gave a final little pat to

the bandage, a touch so light that it might almost have been the hand of that long-dead mother whom I had never known.

"Thank you, yes, very comfortable!" I replied.

"And so your name is Peter Smith, and you are a blacksmith?"

"Yes, a blacksmith."

"And do you live here alone?"

"Quite alone!"

"And how long have you lived here alone?"

"Not so long that I am tired of it."

"And is this cottage yours?"

"Yes. That is, it stands on the Sefton estates, I believe, but nobody hereabouts would dispute my right of occupying the place."

"Why not?"

"Because it is generally supposed to be haunted."

The dark night outside was filled with demons now, who tore at the rattling casements, who roared and bellowed down the chimney.

But here, in the warm firelight, I heeded them not at all, and watched instead this woman, where she sat, leaning forward and gazing deep into the glow.

And where the light touched her hair it awoke strange fires of red and bronze.

It was very rebellious hair, with little tendrils that gleamed, here and there, against her temples, and with small defiant curls that seemed to strive to hide behind her ear, or kiss her snowy neck.

As to her dress, her gown was of a rough, coarse material such as domestic servants wear, but the stockinged feet that peeped at me beneath its hem (her shoes were drying on the hearth) were clad in a silk so fine that I could catch through it the gleam of the white flesh beneath.

From this apparent inconsistency I deduced that she was of educated tastes, but poor—probably a governess, or, more likely still, taking her hands into consideration, with their long, prehensible fingers, a teacher of music.

I was going on to explain to myself her present situation as the outcome of Beauty, Poverty, and the Devil, when she sighed, glanced towards the door, shivered slightly, and reached for her shoes, preparing to slip them on.

"They are still very wet!" I said deprecatingly.

"Yes."

"Listen to the wind; it would be bad travelling for anyone tonight," I said.

Charmian stared into the fire.

"Indeed, it would be madness for the strongest to stir abroad on such a night."

Charmian shivered again.

"And the Inns are all shut, long ago. So it would be pure folly to go."

Charmian continued staring into the fire.

"On the other hand, here is a warm room, and a good fire and a very excellent bed."

She neither spoke nor moved; only her eyes were raised suddenly and swiftly to mine.

"Also," I continued, returning her look, "here, conveniently by your hand, is a fine, sharp knife, in case you are afraid of the ghost or any other midnight visitor—and so good-night, Madam!"

Saying this, I took up one of the candles and crossed to the door of the old room.

Having made the bed, I undressed slowly, pausing frequently to catch the sound of the light, quick footstep beyond the door, and the whisper of her garments as she walked.

"Charmian!" I said to myself, when at length all was still. "Charmian!"

And I blew out my candle. But as I lay in the dark, there came to me a faint perfume like violets, elusive and very sweet, breathing of Charmian herself.

Putting up my hand, I touched the handkerchief that bound my brow.

"Charmian!" I said to myself again, and so fell asleep.

*   *   *

In the early morning things are apt to lose something of the glamour that was theirs at night; so I remained propped up on my elbow, gazing apprehensively at the door.

I was listening for any movement from the room beyond that would tell me she was up, but I heard only the early chorus of the birds, and the gurgle of the brook, swollen with last night's rain.

At last, fully dressed, I sat down to wait until I should hear her footsteps. But I listened vainly, for minute after minute elapsed until, rising at last, I knocked softly. And having knocked three times, each time louder than before, without effect, I lifted the latch and opened the door.

My first glance showed me that the bed had never even been slept in, and that except for myself the place was empty. And yet the breakfast-table had been neatly set, though with only one cup and saucer.

Beside this cup and saucer was one of my few books, and, picking it up, I saw that it was my Virgil. Upon the fly-leaf, where it was open, I had years ago scrawled my name:

PETER VIBART

But close under this, written in a fine Italian hand, were the following words:

To Peter Smith, Esq. Blacksmith Charmian Brown desires to thank Mr. Smith, yet because thanks are so poor and small, and his service so great, needs must she remember him as a gentleman, yet oftener as a blacksmith, and most of all as a man.

Charmian Brown begs him to accept this little trinket in memory of her; it is all she has to offer him. He may also keep her handkerchief.

Upon the table, on the very spot where the book had lain, was a gold heart-shaped locket, very quaint and old-fashioned, upon one side of which was engraved the following posy:

Hee who myne heart would keepe for long
Shall be a gentil man, and strong.

Attached to the locket was a narrow blue ribbon.

Passing this ribbon over my head, I hung the locket about my neck. And having read through the message once more, I closed the Virgil and replaced it on the shelf. Then I sat down to breakfast.

I had scarcely done so, however, when there came a timid knock at the door. I rose expectantly, and immediately sat down again.

"Come in!" I said. The latch was slowly raised, the door swung open, and the Ancient appeared.

"Well, Peter, Black Jarge be 'took' again."

"What?" I exclaimed.

"Oh, I knew it would come—I knew he couldn't last much longer."

"How did it happen, Ancient?"

"Got terrible drunk he did, over at Cranbrook—he threw Mr. Scrope, the beadle, over the churchyard wall—knocked down Jeremy Tullinger, the watchman, and then went to sleep.

"While he was asleep they managed to tie his legs and arms, and locked him up in the vestry. When he woke up he broke the door open and walked out, and nobody tried to stop him—not a soul, Peter."

"And where is he now?"

"Nobody knows, but there's them as says they seen him making for Sefton Woods. Where are you going, Peter?"

"To the forge; there is a lot of work to be done, Ancient."

"But Jarge isn't there to help you."

"Yet the work remains, Ancient."

"Why then, if you are going I'll go with you, Peter."

So, presently we set out together.

I was sitting in the forge, some time later, plunged in a reverie, when a shadow fell across the floor and looking up I saw Prudence.

Her face was troubled and her eyes were red, as from recent tears, while in her hand she held a crumpled paper.

"Mr. Peter . . ." she began, and then stopped, staring at me.

"Well, Prudence?"

"You . . . you've seen him!"

"Him—whom do you mean?"

"Black Jarge!"

"No. What should make you think so?"

"Your face is all cut . . . you've been fighting!"

"And supposing I have? That is none of George's doing; he and I are good friends. Why should we quarrel?"

"Then . . . then it wasn't Jarge?"

"No, I have not seen him since Saturday."

"Thank God! But you must go. Oh, Mr. Peter, I've been so fearful for you, and . . . and . . . you might meet each other anytime, so . . . so you must go away."

"Prudence, what do you mean?"

In answer, she held out the crumpled paper, and scrawled in great straggling characters I read these words:

Prudence,

I'm going away, otherwise I shall kill him, but I shall come back. Tell him not to cross my path or God help him, and you, and me.

George

"You must go soon, he means it. I . . . I've seen death in his face. Go today . . . the longer you stay here, the worse for all of us. . . . Go now!"

"Prudence!"

86

"Yes, Mr. Peter?"

"You always loved Black George, didn't you?"

"Yes, Mr. Peter."

"And you love him still, don't you?"

"Yes, Mr. Peter."

"Excellent! I had always hoped you did, for his sake and for yours, and in my way, a very blundering way as it seems now, I have tried to bring you two together. But things are not hopeless yet. I think I can see a means of straightening out this tangle."

"Oh, if only we could! You see, I was very cruel to him, Mr. Peter!"

"Just a little, perhaps," I said.

While she dabbed at her pretty eyes with her snowy apron, I took a pen and ink from the shelf, which, together with George's letter, I set upon the anvil.

"Now, write down just here, below where George signed his name, what you told me a moment ago."

"You mean that I . . ."

"That you love him, yes."

"Oh, Mr. Peter!"

"Prudence, it is the only way, so far as I can see, of saving George from himself; and no sweet, pure maid need be ashamed to tell her love, especially to such a man as this one, who worships the very ground that those little shoes of yours have once pressed."

She glanced up at me, under her wet lashes,

as I said this, and a soft light beamed in her eyes, and a smile hovered upon her red lips.

"Does he really . . . Mr. Peter?"

"Indeed he does, Prudence, though I think you must know that without my telling you."

So she stooped above the anvil, blushing a little, and wrote these four words:

George, I love you.

"What now, Mr. Peter?"

"Now I am going to look for Black George."

* * *

The moon was rising as, hungry and weary, I came to that steep descent which leads down into the Hollow. And presently I descended into the shadows, and sat down upon a great boulder. Straight away my weariness and hunger were forgotten, and I sat dreaming.

Suddenly I heard a little sound behind me, and, turning my head, I saw someone who stood half in shadow, half in moonlight.

She stood very still, looking half-wistful, as if waiting for me to speak, while from the mysteries of the woods stole the soft, sweet song of a nightingale.

"Charmian?" I said at last, speaking almost in a whisper.

"Charmian!" I repeated. "You—have come, then?"

"Were you expecting me?"

"I ... I think I was ... that is ... I ... I don't know!"

"Then you are not very surprised to see me?"

"No."

"And you are not ... very sorry to see me?"

"No."

"And ... are you not very glad to see me?"

"Yes."

Here there fell a silence between us.

"When I went away this morning," she began at last, "I didn't think I should ever come back again."

"No, I supposed not."

"But, you see, I had no money."

"And there was three pounds, fifteen shillings, and sixpence in my old shoe," I said.

"Sevenpence!"

"Sevenpence?"

"Three pounds, fifteen shillings, and sevenpence. I counted it."

"Oh! Three pounds, fifteen shillings, and sevenpence is not a great sum, but perhaps it will enable you to reach your family."

"I'm afraid not. You see, I have no family."

"Your friends, then."

"I have no friends; I am alone in the world. I have neither friends nor family nor money, and so, being hungry, I came back here and ate up all the bacon."

Now, as she stood, half in shadow, half in moonlight, I could not help but be conscious of her loveliness.

"Indeed," I said, speaking my thoughts aloud, "this is no place for a woman."

"No," she said very softly.

"No, although, certainly, there are worse places."

"Yes," she replied, "I suppose so."

"Then," I said, "if you are friendless, God forbid that I should refuse you the shelter of even such a place as this—so, if you are homeless and without money, stay here, if you want to—as long as it pleases you."

I kept my eyes directed to the running water at my feet, as I waited for her answer, and it seemed a very long time before she spoke.

"Are you fond of stewed rabbit?"

"Rabbit!"

"With onions!"

"Onions?"

"I can cook a little, and supper is waiting."

"Supper?"

"So, if you are hungry . . ."

"I am ravenous!"

"Then why not come home and eat it?"

"Home?"

"Instead of echoing my words . . . come!"

She turned and led the way to the cottage. And behold, the candles were lit, the table was spread with a snowy cloth, and a pot simmered upon the hob; a pot that gave forth a delectable odour, and into which she gazed with an anxious frown.

"I think it's all right!"

"I'm sure of it; but please, where did you get it?"

"I bought this for sixpence ... out of the old shoe."

"Sixpence? Then they were certainly poached. These are in the Cambourne Woods, and everything within them—fish, flesh, or fowl, living or dead—belongs to the Lady Sophia Sefton of Cambourne."

"Then ... perhaps we had better not eat it," she said, glancing at me over her shoulder. But, meeting my eye, she laughed.

And so presently we sat down to supper, and, poached though it may have been, that rabbit made a truly noble meal.

＊　　＊　　＊

We were walking in the moonlight.

"Let us talk about ourselves," Charmian suggested.

"As you please."

"Very well, you begin."

"Well, I am a blacksmith."

"Yes, you told me so before."

"And I make horseshoes. . . ."

"He is a blacksmith, and makes horseshoes!" Charmian said, nodding at the moon.

"Then let us talk of something else."

"Yes," she agreed, "let us talk of the woman Charmian . . . Charmian Brown."

A tress of hair had come loose, and hung low above her brow, and in its shadow her eyes seemed more elusive, more mocking, than ever. And, while our glances met, she put up a hand and began to wind this glossy tress round and round her finger.

"Well?" she said. "What do you think of Charmian Brown?"

"I think of her as little as I can."

"Indeed, Sir!"

"Indeed," I replied.

"And why, pray?"

"Because," I said, knocking the ashes from my pipe. "Because the more I think about her the more incomprehensible she becomes."

There was a long silence.

"Talking of Charmian Brown . . ." I began.

"Do you really wish to hear about that . . . humble person?"

"Very much!"

"Then you must know, in the first place, that she is old, Sir, dreadfully old!"

"But she really cannot be more than twenty-three—or -four at the most."

"She is just twenty-one!" returned Charmian, rather hastily, I thought.

"Quite a child!"

"No, indeed it is experience that ages one, and by experience she is quite two hundred!"

"Very well, then; continue, please."

"Now, this woman," Chairman went on, beginning to curl the tress of hair again, "hating the world about her with its shams, its hypocrisy, and cruelty, ran away from it all one day with a villain."

"And why with a villain?"

"*Because* he was a villain!"

"That I do not understand!"

"No, I didn't suppose you would."

"Hum!" I said, rubbing my chin. "And why did you run away *from* him?"

"Because he *was* a villain."

Here there fell a lengthy silence between us, and as we walked, now and then her gown would brush my knee or her shoulder touch mine, for the path was very narrow.

"And—did you . . ."

"Did I . . . what, Sir?"

"Did you love him?"

"I . . . ran away from him."

"And—do you—love him?"

"I suppose you cannot understand a woman hating and loving a man, admiring and despising him, both at the same time?"

"No, I can't."

"Can you understand one glorying in the tempest that may destroy her, riding a fierce horse that may crush her, or being attracted by a will strong, and masterful, before which all must yield or break?"

"I think I can."

"Then this man is strong, and wild, and very masterful, and so . . . I ran away with him."

"And do you—love him?"

"I . . . don't know."

After this we fell silent altogether, yet once, when I happened to glance at her, I saw that her eyes were very bright beneath the shadow of her drooping lashes, and that her lips were smiling; and I pondered very deeply as to why this should be.

Re-entering the cottage, I closed the door, and waited while she lit my candle.

And, having taken the candle from her hand, I bade her good-night, but paused at the door of my chamber.

"You feel quite safe here?"

"Quite safe!"

"Despite the colour of my hair and eyes—you have no fear of—Peter Smith?"

"None!"

"Because he is neither fierce nor wild, nor masterful!"

"Because he is neither fierce nor wild."

"Nor masterful!"

"Nor masterful!" Charmian said, averting her head.

So I opened the door, but even then felt compelled to turn back again.

"Do you think I am so very different—from *him?*"

"As different as day from night, as the lamb from the wolf," she said, without looking at me. "Good-night, Peter!"

"Good-night!" I said; and, going into my room, I closed the door behind me.

"A lamb!" I said, tearing off my neckcloth, and sat for some time listening to her footstep and the soft rustle of her petticoats going to and fro.

"A lamb!" I said, for the third time, but at this moment there came a light tap at the door.

"Yes?" I said, without moving.

"Oh, how is your injured thumb?"

"Thank you, it is as well as can be expected."

"Does it hurt you very much?"

"It is not unbearable!" I said.

"Good-night, Peter!" And I heard her move away. But presently she was back again.

"Oh, Peter?"

"Well?"

"Are you frowning?"

"I think I was—why?"

"When you frown, you are very like *him,* and

95

have the same square set of the mouth and chin when you are angry ... so don't, please don't frown ... Peter. ... Good-night!"

"Good-night, Charmian!" I said; and, stooping, I picked up the little handkerchief and thrust it under my pillow.

Chapter
Five

I was working in the garden when a peddler chanced to go by and, seeing me at work, stopped to pass the time of day.

He was a talkative man, like many of his kind, and on my enquiring kindly if he was married, he treated me to a discourse on the fickleness of women.

"Don't talk to me of women, my chap, I can't abide 'em—bah! If there's any trouble afoot, you may take your Bible oath that there's a woman about somewhere—there always is!"

"Do you think so?"

"I knows so; I am hearing and seeing such all day and every day—there's Black Jarge, for one."

"What about him?"

"What about him!" repeated the peddler.

"Why, hasn't his life been ruined, broke, worn away by one of them Eves?"

"What do you mean—how has his life been ruined?"

"Oh, the usual way of it; Jarge loves a girl, the girl loves Jarge—sugar ain't sweeter, you might say. Then along comes another man, a man with nice white hands and soft, taking ways—he talks with her, walks with her, smiles at her—and poor Jarge isn't anywhere!"

"How do you come to know all this?"

"How should I come to know it but from the man himself?"

"And when did he tell you all this?"

"This morning."

"Where did you see him?"

"The runners is after him, looking for him high and low, and though I'm married, I ain't one to give a man away. I ain't a friendly man myself, but I like Black Jarge—I pities and despises him."

"Why do you despise him?"

"Because he carries on so, all about an Eve. There ain't a woman breathing as is worth a man's troubling his head over, no, nor ever will be. Yet here's Black Jarge ready and, ah, more than willing to get himself hung and all for a wench —an Eve. . . ."

"Get himself hung?"

"Yes, hung! Isn't he waiting to get at this

man—this man with the nice white hands and the taking ways. Isn't he watching to meet him some lonely night—and when he does meet him . . ."

The peddler sighed.

"Well?"

"Why, there will be bloodshed—blood—quarts of it—buckets of it."

At that moment Charmian appeared, and the peddler fell back three or four paces, staring with round eyes.

"By golly!" he exclaimed. "So you are married, then?"

Now, when he said this I felt suddenly hot all over, and for the life of me I could not have looked at Charmian.

"No . . . he is not married," she said, "far from it."

"Not?" the peddler said. "So much the better; marriage isn't love, no, nor love isn't marriage—I'm a married man myself, so I know what I'm talking about."

"Come—get away!" I said angrily.

"What, are you going to turn me away, at this time of night?"

"It is not so far to Sissinghurst!" I replied.

"But Lord! I wouldn't disturb you—and there's two rooms, isn't there?"

"There are plenty of comfortable beds to be had at the Bull."

"Very well then," he shouted. "I hopes as you gets your head knocked off! Ah! And gets it knocked off soon!"

Having said this, he spat up into the air towards me and trudged off.

Hearing a laugh behind me, I turned and saw that Charmian was leaning in the open doorway, watching me.

"And so you are the ... the man ... with the white hands and the taking ways, are you, Peter?"

"Why—you were actually—listening, then?"

"Why, of course I was."

"That was very undignified!"

"But very ... feminine, Peter. Poor, poor Black George!" she said, and sighed.

"What do you mean by that?"

"Really, I can almost understand his being angry with you."

"Why?"

"You walked with her and talked with her, Peter, and even smiled at her, Peter ... and you so rarely smile!"

Having struck flint and steel several times without success, I thrust the tinder-box back into my pocket and fixed my gaze upon the moon.

"Is she pretty, Peter?"

I stared up at the moon without answering.

Presently, finding that I would not speak, Charmian began to sing, very sweet and low, as if to herself, yet when I chanced to glance towards her, I found her mocking eyes still watching me.

At last, unable to bear it any longer, I rose, and taking my candle went into my room and closed the door. But I had been there scarcely five minutes when Charmian knocked.

"Oh, Peter, I wish to speak to you, please."

"What is it, Charmian?"

"You dropped this from your pocket when you took out your tinder-box so clumsily!" she said, holding towards me a crumpled paper.

And looking down at it I saw that it was Black George's letter to Prudence.

Now, as I took it from her, I noticed that her hand trembled, while in her eyes I read fear and trouble. And seeing this, I was for a brief moment glad, and then wondered at myself.

"You—did not read it—of course?" I said, well knowing that she had.

"Yes, Peter . . . it lay open, and . . ."

"Then you know that she loves George."

"He means to harm you," she said, speaking with her head averted, "and if he killed you . . ."

"There is no chance of such a thing happening—not the remotest. Black George's bark is a thousand times worse than his bite. This letter means nothing, and—er—nothing at all."

She had turned and was looking at me over her shoulder.

"If he has to 'wait and wait and follow you, and follow you'?" she said, in the same low tone.

"Those are merely the words of a half-mad peddler."

"And your blood will go soaking, and soaking into the grass!"

"Our peddler has a vivid imagination!" I said lightly.

But she shook her head, and turned to look out upon the beauty of the night once more, while I watched her, chin in hand.

"Your hand is very small," I said, finding nothing better to say, "smaller even than I had thought."

"Is it?" And she smiled and glanced up at me beneath her lashes, for her head was still bent.

"And wonderfully smooth and soft!"

"Is it?" she said again, but this time she did not look up at me.

Now another man might have stooped and kissed those slender, shapely fingers—but, as for me, I loosened them, rather suddenly, and once more bidding her good-night, re-entered my own room and closed the door.

But tonight, lying upon my bed, I could not sleep and instead I lay there watching the luminous patch of sky framed in my open casement.

I thought of Charmian, of her beauty, of her strange whims and fancies, her swift-changing moods, and her contrariness, comparing her, in turn, to all those fair women I had ever read of or dreamed over in my books.

Little by little, however, my thoughts drifted to Black George, and with my mind's eye I could see him as he was, fierce-eyed and grim of mouth, sitting beneath some hedgerow while, knife in hand, he trimmed and trimmed his two bludgeons, one of which was to batter the life out of me.

* * *

Charmian sighed, bit the end of her pen, and sighed again. She was deep in her housekeeping accounts, adding and subtracting, and, between this, regarding the result with a rueful frown.

"What is it, Charmian?"

"Compound addition, Peter, and I hate figures. I detest, loathe, and abominate them ... especially when they won't balance!"

"Then never mind them," I said.

"Never mind them then, the very idea! How can I help minding them when living costs so much and we are so poor?"

"Are we?"

"Why, of course we are."

"Yes, to be sure, I suppose we are," I said dreamily.

"We have spent nine shillings and tenpence, Peter!"

"Good, indeed!"

"Leaving exactly . . . two pence over."

"A penny for you and a penny for me."

"I fear I am a very bad housekeeper, Peter."

"On the contrary."

"But you work so very, very hard, and earn so little . . . and that little . . ."

"I work that I may live, Charmian, and I am alive."

"And dreadfully poor!"

"And ridiculously happy."

"I wonder why," she said, beginning to draw designs on the page before her.

"Upon consideration, I think my thanks are due to my uncle for dying and leaving me penniless."

"Do you mean that he disinherited you?"

"In a way, yes; he left me his whole fortune provided that I marry a certain lady within the year."

"A certain lady?"

"The Lady Sophia Sefton of Cambourne."

Charmian's pen stopped in the very middle of a letter, and she bent down to examine what she had been writing.

"Oh! The Lady Sophia Sefton of Cambourne?"

"Yes."

"And . . . your cousin . . . Sir Maurice . . . were the conditions the same in his case?"

"Precisely!"

"Oh! And this lady . . . she will not . . . marry you?"

"No."

"Are you quite . . . sure?"

"Certain—you see, I never intend to ask her."

Charmian suddenly raised her head and looked at me.

"Why not, Peter?"

"Because, should I ever marry—a remote contingency, and most improbable—I am sufficiently self-willed to prefer to exert my own choice in the matter; moreover, this lady is a celebrated toast." I paused to say positively: "It would be most repugnant to me that my wife's name should ever have been bandied from mouth to mouth, and hiccoughed out over slopping wine-glasses. . . ."

The pen slipped from Charmian's fingers to the floor, and before I could pick it up she had forestalled me, so that when she raised her head she was flushed with stooping.

"Have you ever seen this lady, Peter?"

"Never, but I have heard of her—who has not?"

"What have you heard?"

"That she galloped her horse up and down the steps of Saint Paul's Cathedral, for one thing."

"What else?"

"That she is proud, and passionate, and with a quick temper—in a word, a virago!"

105

"Virago!" said Charmian, flinging up her head.

"Virago! Though she is handsome, I understand, in a strapping way, and I have it on very excellent authority that she is a black-browed goddess, a peach, and a veritable plum."

" 'Strappin' is a hateful word, Peter!"

"But very descriptive."

"And . . . doesn't she interest you . . . a little, Peter?"

"Not in the least."

"And pray, why not?"

"Because I care very little for either peaches or plums."

"Or black-browed goddesses, Peter?"

"Not if she is big and strapping, and possesses a temper."

"I suppose . . . to such a philosopher as you . . . a woman or a goddess, black-browed or not, can scarcely compare with, or hope to rival, an old book, can she?"

"Why, that depends, Charmian."

"On what?"

"On the book!"

Charmian rested her round elbows upon the table and, setting her chin in her hands, stared squarely at me.

"Peter."

"Yes, Charmian?"

"If ever you did meet this lady . . . I think . . ."

106

"Well?"

"I know . . ."

"What?"

"That you would fall a very easy victim!"

"I think not," I said.

"You would be her slave in a month, three weeks, or much less. . . ."

"Preposterous!"

"If she set herself to make you!"

"That would be very immodest! Besides, no woman can make a man love her."

"Do your books teach you that, Peter?"

Here, finding I did not answer, she laughed and nodded her head at me.

"You would be head over ears in love before you knew it!"

"I think not!"

"You are the kind of man who would grow sick with love and never know what ailed him."

"Any man in such a condition would be a pitiful ass!"

Charmian only laughed at me again, and went back to her scribbling.

"Then, if this lady married you, you would be a gentleman of good position and standing?"

"Yes, I suppose so—and probably miserable."

"And rich, Peter?"

"I should have more than enough."

"Instead of being a village blacksmith . . ."

"With just enough, and absurdly happy and

content, which is far more desirable—at least I think so."

"Do you mean to say that you would rather exist here, and make horseshoes all your life, than ... live, respected and rich?"

"And married to ..."

"And married to the Lady Sophia?"

"Infinitely!"

"Then your cousin, so far as you are concerned, is free to woo and win her and your uncle's fortune?"

"And I wish him well of his bargain!" I nodded. "As for me, I shall probably continue to live here, and make horseshoes—wifeless and content."

"Is marriage so hateful to you?"

"In the Abstract—no; for in my mind there exists a woman whom I think I could love—very greatly. But in the Actual, yes, because there is no woman in all the world that is like this woman of my mind."

"Is she so flawlessly perfect ... this imaginary woman?"

"She is one whom I would respect for her intellect."

"Yes."

"Whom I would honour for her proud virtue."

"Yes, Peter."

"Whom I would worship for her broad charity, her gentleness, and her spotless purity."

"Yes, Peter."

"And love with all my strength, for her warm, sweet womanhood—in a word, she is the epitome of all that is true and womanly!"

"And of course this imaginary creature of yours is ethereal, bloodless, sexless, unnatural, and quite impossible!"

Now, when she spoke like this, I laid down my pipe and stared, but before I could get my breath she began again, with curling lips and lashes that drooped disdainfully.

"I quite understand that there can be no woman worthy of Mr. Peter Vibart . . . she whom he would honour with marriage must be specially created for him!"

She paused, then continued:

"Ah, but someday a woman, a real, live woman, will come into his life, and the touch of her hand, the glance of her eyes, the warmth of her breath, will dispel this poor, misty creature of his imagination; she will fade and fade, and vanish into nothingness."

Her voice deepened with scorn.

"And when this real woman has shown him how utterly false and impossible this dream woman was . . . then, Mr. Peter Vibart, I hope she will laugh at you . . . as I do, and turn her back upon you . . . as I do, and leave you . . . for the very superior, very pedantic pedant that you are, and scorn you . . . as I do, most of all because you are merely a . . . creature!"

With the word she flung up her head and stamped her foot at me, and turning, swept out through the open door and into the moonlight.

"Creature?" I said, and sat staring at the table in blank amazement.

But after a while I went and stood in the doorway, looking at Charmian but saying nothing.

As I watched, she began to sing softly to herself, and, putting up her hand, drew the comb from her hair so that it fell down, rippling about her neck and shoulders.

"Charmian, you have glorious hair!" I said, speaking on impulse—a thing I rarely do.

But Charmian only combed her tresses and went on singing to herself.

"Charmian, what did you mean when you called me a—creature? I fear my manner must be very unfortunate to give you such an opinion of me."

Charmian went on singing.

"Naturally, I am rather perturbed, and doubly anxious to know what you wish me to understand by the epithet 'creature'."

Charmian went on singing.

So, seeing she did not intend to answer me, I presently re-entered the cottage.

Now, it is my custom, when at all troubled or put out in any way, to seek consolation in my books; hence, I took up my Homer and, trimming the candles, sat down at the table.

In a little while Charmian came in, still humming the air of her song, and didn't even glance in my direction.

Some days before, at her request, I had brought her linen and lace and ribands from Cranbrook, and she took these out, together with a needle and cotton, and, sitting down at the opposite side of the table, began to sew.

She was still humming, and this in itself distracted my mind from the lines before me. Moreover, my eye was fascinated by the gleam of her flying needle, and I began to debate within myself what she was making.

Glancing up suddenly, she caught my eye, and for no reason in the world I felt suddenly guilty. To hide this I began to search through my pockets for my pipe.

"On the mantelshelf!" she said.

"What is?"

"Your pipe!"

"Thank you!" I said, and took it down.

"What are you reading?" she enquired. "Is it about Helen, or Aspasia or Phryne?"

"Neither, it is the parting of Hector and Andromache," I answered.

"Is it very interesting?"

"Yes."

"Then why do your eyes wander so often from the page?"

"I know many of the lines by heart," I said.

And, having lit my pipe, I took up the book and once more began to read.

Charmian continued to sew industriously, and I went forth with brave Hector to face the mighty Achilles. But my eye had traversed barely twenty lines when:

"Peter?"

"Yes?"

"Do you remember my giving you a locket?"

"Yes."

"Where is it?"

"Oh! I have it still—somewhere."

"Somewhere!" she repeated, glancing at me with raised brows.

"Somewhere safe," I said, fixing my eyes upon my book.

"It had a ribbon attached, hadn't it?"

"Yes."

"A pink ribbon, if I remember—yes, pink."

"No—it was blue!" I said unguardedly.

"Are you sure, Peter?"

Glancing up, I saw that she was watching me beneath her lashes.

"Yes, that is—I think so."

"Then you are not sure?"

"Yes, I am," I said, "it was a blue ribbon."

I turned over a page very ostentatiously.

"Oh!" Charmian said, and there was another pause.

"Peter?"

"Well?"

"Where did you say it was now...my locket?"

"I didn't say it was anywhere."

"No, you said it was 'somewhere'...in a rather vague sort of way, Peter."

"Well, perhaps I did," I said, frowning at my book.

"It is not very valuable, but I prized it for association's sake, Peter."

"Ah! yes, to be sure."

"I was wondering if you ever...wear it, Peter?"

"Wear it!" I exclaimed, and glancing furtively down at myself, I was relieved to see that there were no signs of a betraying blue ribbon.

"Wear it!" I said again. "Why should I wear it?"

"Why, indeed, Peter, unless it was because it was there to wear."

Suddenly she uttered an exclamation of annoyance and, taking up a candle, began looking about the floor.

"What have you lost?"

"My needle! I think it must have fallen under the table. Won't you please help me to find it?"

"With pleasure!" I said, getting down upon my hands and knees, and together we began to hunt for the lost needle.

113

Now, in our search it chanced that we drew near together, and once her hand touched mine, and once her soft hair brushed my cheek.

There stole over me a perfume like the breath of violets, the fragrance that I always associated with her, faint and sweet and alluring—so much so that I drew back from further chance of contact, and kept my eyes directed to the floor.

And, after I had searched vainly for some time, I raised my head and looked at Charmian, to find her regarding me with a very strange expression.

"What is it? Have you found the needle?"

Charmian sat back on her heels and laughed softly.

"Oh yes, I've found the needle, Peter, but then—I never lost it."

"Why then—what—what do you mean?"

For answer she raised her hand and pointed to my breast.

Then, glancing hurriedly down, I saw that the locket had slipped forward through my shirt and hung in plain view. I made an instinctive movement to hide it, but, hearing her laugh, looked at her instead.

"So that is why you asked me to stoop to find your needle?"

"Yes, Peter."

"Then you—knew?"

"Of course I knew."

"Hum!" I said.

A distant clock chimed eleven, and Charmian began to fold away her work, and seeing this, I rose and took up my candle.

"And pray," I said, staring hard at the flame of my candle, "how did you happen to find out?"

"Very simply ... I saw the ribbon round your neck days ago. Good-night, Peter!"

"Oh," I said. "Good-night!"

*   *   *

"Lord love me!"

I plunged the iron back into the fire, and, turning my head, saw a figure standing in the doorway. Although the leather hat and short, round jacket had been superseded by a smart groom's livery, I recognised the postillion I had met on the night Charmian came to me.

"Well, if it don't beat everything as ever I heard!"

"What do you mean?"

"I means my dropping in on you like this, just as if you wasn't the one man in all England as I was hopeful to drop in on."

"Were you sent to find me?"

"Easy a bit—you're a blacksmith, aren't you?"

"I told you so before."

"What's more, you looks a blacksmith in that there leather apron, and with your face all smutty. To be sure, you're powerful like him—Number One as was—my master as now is—and this brings me round to her!"

"Her?"

"Yes—her! Number Two—her as quarrelled with Number One all the way from London—her as ran away from Number One—what about her?"

And as I watched him it seemed to me that this was the question that had been in his mind all along.

"Seeing she did manage to run away from him—Number One—she is probably very well."

"Ah, to be sure! Very well, you say? Where might she be now?"

"That I am unable to tell you," I said, and began to blow up the fire while the postillion watched me, sucking the handle of his whip reflectively.

"You work uncommonly hard—drown me if you don't!"

"Pretty hard!"

"And gets well paid for it, perhaps?"

"Not so well as I could wish."

"Well, how much might you be getting a week?"

"Ten shillings."

"Gets ten shillings a week!" He nodded to the sledgehammer. "That isn't much for a chap like him."

"Well?"

"Well," he said, fixing his eye upon the bellows again, "supposing you was to make a guinea over and above your wages this week?"

"You must speak more plainly."

"Well then, supposing I was to place a guinea down on that there anvil of yours, would that help you to remember where Number Two might be?"

"No!"

"It wouldn't?"

"No."

"Then say—oh! two pounds ten and have done with it."

"No!"

"What—not—do you say no to two pounds ten?"

"I do."

"Well, let's say three pounds."

I shook my head, and, drawing the iron from the fire, began to hammer at it.

"Well then," shouted the postillion, for I was making as much din as possible, "say four—five —ten—fifteen—twenty-five—fifty!"

Here I ceased hammering.

"Tell me when you've done!"

"You're a cool customer, you are—I never seen a cooler one!"

"Other people have thought the same," I said, examining the half-finished horseshoe before setting it back in the fire.

"Sixty guineas!"

"Come again!"

"Seventy then!"

"Once more!"

"A hundred—one hundred guineas!" he said, removing his hat to mop at his brow.

"Any more?"

"No!" retorted the postillion sulkily, putting on his hat. "I'm done!"

"Did he set the figure at a hundred guineas?"

"Him—oh! He's mad for her, he is—he'd ruin himself, body and soul, for her, he would, but I ain't going to offer no more. No woman as ever breathed is worth more than a hundred guineas."

"Then I wish you good-day!"

"But—just think—a hundred guineas is a fortune!"

"Let me fully understand you then. You propose to pay me one hundred guineas on behalf of your master, known as Number One, for such information as shall enable him to discover the whereabouts of a certain person known as her, Number Two—is that how the matter stands?"

"Ah! That's how it stands. The money to be yours as soon as ever he lays hands on her—is it a go?"

"No!"

"No?"

"No!"

"Why, you must be stark, staring mad—that you must—unless you're sweet on her yourself. . . ."

I made towards him, but he darted nimbly to

118

the door, where, seeing that I did not pursue, he paused.

"I may be a fool, but I don't go falling in love with ladies that are above me and out of my reach, and don't chuck away a hundred guineas for one as ain't likely to look my way—not me!"

With which he set his thumb to his nose, spread out his fingers, wagged them, and swaggered off.

Above me and out of my reach! One not likely to look my way!

And, in due course, having finished the horseshoe, I took my hat and coat and set out for the Hollow.

＊　＊　＊

It was evening—that time before the moon is up and when the earth is dark and full of shadows. Now, as I went, by some chance there came to me the words of an old song I had read somewhere, the song of an old love-sick poet.

The words of the old song recurred again and again, pathetically insistent, voicing themselves in my footsteps, so that to banish them I presently stood still.

And in that very moment a gigantic figure came bursting through the hedge, clearing the ditch in a single bound—and Black George confronted me.

Haggard of face, with hair and beard matted and unkempt, his clothes all dusty and torn, he presented a very wild and terrible appearance; and beneath one arm he carried two bludgeons.

For a moment neither of us spoke, only we looked at each other steadily in the eye, and I saw the hair of his beard bristle, and he raised one great hand to the collar of his shirt, and tore it open as if it were strangling him.

"George!" I said at last, and held out my hand.

George never stirred.

"Won't you shake hands, George?"

His lips opened but no words came.

"Had I known where to look for you, I should have sought you out days ago. As it is, I have been wishing to meet you, hoping to set matters right."

Once again his lips opened, but still no word came.

"You see, Prudence is breaking her heart over you."

A laugh burst from him, sudden and harsh.

"You're a liar!"

"I speak gospel truth!"

"I be nothing to Prue—and you know it."

"Prudence loves you and always has! Go back to her, George, go back to her, and to your work—be the man I know you are, go back to her—she loves you. If you still doubt my word—here, read that!"

And I held out his own letter, the letter on

which Prudence had written those four words: "George, I love you."

He took it from me, crumpled it slowly in his hand, and tossed it into the ditch.

"You're a liar," he said again, "and a—coward!"

"And you," I said, "you are a fool, a blind, selfish fool, who, in degrading yourself—in skulking about the woods and lanes—is bringing black shame and sorrow to as sweet a maid as ever . . ."

"It don't need you to tell me what she is and what she isn't," said Black George in a low, repressed voice.

"I knew her long afore you ever set eyes on her—grew up with her, I did, and I aren't deaf nor blind. You see, I loved her all my life—that's why one of us two's going to lie out here all night —ah! and all tomorrow, also, if someone doesn't find us."

Then he forced a cudgel into my hand.

"But why?" I cried. "In God's name, why?"

"I be slow, perhaps, and thick perhaps, but I am not a fool—come, man—if she be worth winning, she be worth fighting for."

"But I tell you she loves Black George and no other—she never had any thought of me, nor I of her. This is madness!" And I tossed the cudgel aside.

"And I tell you—you're a shame to the woman who loves you and the woman that bore you. Stand up, I say, or by God I'll do it for you!"

And he raised his weapon.

Without another word I picked up the cudgel, and, pointing to a gate a little farther along the road, I led the way into the meadow beyond.

I couldn't help thinking that supper would be ready and Charmian would be waiting for me just about now, and I sighed as I drew off my coat and laid it, together with my hat, under the hedge.

And as I stooped and gripped my weapon I remembered how I had that morning kissed her fingers, and I was strangely comforted and glad.

The night air, which had been warm, suddenly struck chilly now, and as I stood up in front of Black George I shivered.

Seeing this, he laughed and came at me, striking downwards at my hand as he came, and tough wood met tough wood with a shock that jarred me from wrist to shoulder.

To hit him upon the arm and disable him was my one thought and object. I therefore watched for an opening, parrying his swift strokes and avoiding his rushes as well as I could.

Time and time again our weapons crashed together. I was already bruised in half-a-dozen places; my right hand and arm felt numb, and with a shooting pain in the shoulder that grew more acute with every movement; my breath also was beginning to labour.

Yet still Black George pressed on, untiring, relentless, showering blow on blow, while my arm grew ever weaker and weaker, and the pain in my shoulder throbbed more intensely.

How long had we fought? Five minutes—ten—half-an-hour—an hour?

"George," I said.

"You're bleeding, Peter!"

"For that matter, so are you. Have we not bled each other sufficiently?"

"No," cried George, between set teeth. "There is more between you and me. Didn't I say as how one of us would be laid out here all night—and so you shall—come on, by God! Fists will be better, after all."

This was the heyday of boxing, and while at Oxford I had earned some small fame at the sport. But it was one thing to spar with a man my own weight in a padded ring, with limited rounds covered by a code of rules, and quite another to fight a man like Black George, in a lonely meadow, by moonlight.

But, as the fight progressed I found that I was far the quicker, as I had hoped, and that the majority of his blows I either blocked or avoided easily enough.

I fought desperately now, yet his blows had four times the weight of mine. My forearms were bruised to either elbow, and my breath came in gasps, and always I watched that deadly "right."

Presently it came, with arm and shoulder and body behind it—quick as a flash, and resistless as a cannon-ball. But I was ready, and as I leaped I struck, and struck him clean and true upon the angle of the jaw; and spinning round, Black George fell, lying with his arms wide stretched, his face buried in the grass.

Slowly he got to his knees, and then to his feet, and so stood, panting, bruised, cut, and disfigured, staring at me.

Now, as I looked, my heart went out to him and I reached forth my right hand.

"George!" I panted. "Oh, George!"

But Black George only looked at me, and shook his head and groaned.

"Oh, Peter!" he said. "You are a man, Peter! No man ever knocked me down before. Oh, Peter, I could love you for it, if I didn't hate the very sight of you. Come on, and let's get it over and done with."

So once again fists were clenched and jaws set—once again came the trampling of feet, the hiss of breath, and the thudding shocks of blows given and taken.

A sudden, jarring impact—the taste of sulphur on my tongue—a gathering darkness before my eyes; and, knowing this was the end, I strove desperately to close with him. But I was dazed, blind—my arms felt paralysed, and in that moment the smith's right fist drove forward.

A jagged flame shot up to Heaven—the earth seemed to rush up towards me—a roaring blackness engulfed me, and then—silence.

Someone was calling to me from a long way off.

"Peter . . . speak to me, Peter!"

'Charmian?' I said, within myself. 'Why, truly, whose hand but hers could have lifted me out of that gulf of death, back to light and life?'

"Ah! Speak to me . . . speak to me, Peter! How can you lie there so still and pale?"

And now her arms were about me, strong and protecting, and my head was drawn down upon her bosom.

"Oh, Peter . . . my Peter!"

No, but was this Charmian, the cold, proud Charmian! Truly I had never heard that thrill in her voice before; could this indeed be Charmian?

And lying thus, with my head on this sweet pillow, I could hear her heart whispering to me, and it seemed that it was striving to tell me something, striving, striving to tell me something, could I but understand! Ah! Could I but understand!

"I waited for you so long, and . . . the supper is all spoiled, a rabbit, Peter . . . you liked rabbit, and . . . and, oh, God! I want you . . . don't you hear me, Peter . . . I want you . . . want you!"

Now her cheek was pressed to mine, and her lips were upon my hair and upon my brow—her lips! Was this indeed Charmian, and was I Peter Vibart?

Ah, if I could but know what it was her

heart was trying to tell me so quickly and passionately!

And while I lay, listening, something hot splashed down upon my cheek, and then another, and another. Her bosom heaved tumultuously; and, instinctively raising my arms, I clasped them about her.

"Don't!" I said, and my voice was a whisper. "Don't, Charmian!"

For a moment her clasp tightened about me, and she was all tenderness and clinging warmth, then I heard a sudden gasp, and her arms loosened and fell away.

So I presently raised my head and, supporting myself upon my hand, looked at her. And then I saw that her cheeks were burning.

"Peter."

"Yes, Charmian?"

"Did you . . ."

She paused, plucking nervously at the grass, and looking away from me.

"Well, Charmian?"

"Did you . . . hear . . ."

Again she broke off, and still her head was averted.

"I heard your voice calling to me from a great way off, and so—I came, Charmian."

"Were you conscious when . . . when I found you?"

"No," I answered; "I was lying in a very deep, black pit."

Here she looked at me again.

"I . . . I thought you were dead, Peter."

"My soul was out of my body, until you re-called it."

"You were lying upon your back, by the hedge here, and . . . oh, Peter! Your face was white and shining in the moonlight . . . and there was . . . blood upon it, and you looked like one who is . . . dead!"

She shivered.

"And you have brought me back to life," I said, rising; but, being upon my feet, I staggered giddily, to hide which I laughed, and leaned against a tree.

"Indeed, I am very much alive still, and monstrously hungry—you spoke of a rabbit, I think. . . ."

"A rabbit!" said Charmian in a whisper, and as I met her eyes I would have given much to have recalled that thoughtless speech.

"I—I think you did mention a rabbit," I said, floundering deeper.

"So then . . . you deceived me, you lay there and deceived me . . . with your eyes shut, and your ears open, taking advantage of my pity. . . ."

"No, no—I thought myself still dreaming; it —it all seemed so unreal, so—so beyond all be-lief and possibility, and . . ."

I stopped, aghast at my folly, for with a cry she sprang to her feet and hid her face in her hands, while I stood dumbfounded like the fool

I was. When she looked up, her eyes seemed to scorch me.

"And I thought Mr. Vibart a man of honour ... like a Knight of his old-time romances, high and chivalrous.... Oh! I thought him a gentleman!"

"Instead of which you find me only a blacksmith, a low, despicable fellow, eager to take advantage of your unprotected womanhood."

She did not speak, standing tall and straight, her head thrown back.

"And yet this despicable blacksmith fellow refused one hundred guineas for you today."

"Peter!" she cried, and shrank away from me as if I had threatened to strike her.

"Ah! You start at that—your proud lip trembles. Do not fear that the sum did not tempt him —though a large one."

"Peter!" she cried again, and now there was a note of appeal in her voice.

"Indeed, even so degraded a fellow as this blacksmith could not very well sell that which he does not possess—could he? And so the hundred guineas goes begging, and you are still—unsold!"

Long before I had finished she had covered her face again, and, coming near, I saw the tears running out between her fingers and sparkling as they fell.

"Charmian! Forgive me—you will, you must!"

Kneeling before her, I strove to catch her gown, and kiss its hem, but she drew it close

128

about her, and turning fled from me through the shadows.

Heedless of all else but that she was leaving me, I stumbled to my feet and followed.

The trees seemed to beset me as I ran, and rushed to reach out arms to stay me, but I burst from them, running wildly, blunderingly, for she was going—Charmian was leaving me.

And so, spent and panting, I reached the cottage, and met Charmian at the door. She was clad in the long cloak she had worn when she came, and the hood was drawn close about her face.

I stood panting in the doorway, barring her exit.

"Let me pass, Peter."

"By God—no!" I cried; and, entering, closed the door and leaned my back against it.

And after we had stood awhile, looking at each other, I reached out my hands to her, and my hands were torn and bloody.

"Don't go, Charmian, don't go! Ch-Charmian, I'm hurt—I didn't want you to know, but you mustn't leave me—I am not well, it is my head, I think. I met Black George, and he was too strong for me. I'm deaf, Charmian, and half-blinded— oh, don't leave me—I'm afraid, Charmian!"

Her figure grew more blurred and I sank down upon my knees; but in the dimness I reached out and found her hands, and clasped them, and bowed my aching head upon them, and remained thus a great while, as it seemed to me.

And presently, through the mist, her voice reached me.

"Oh, Peter! I will not leave you ... lean on me ... there ... there!"

And little by little, those strong, gentle hands drew me up once more to light and life. And so she got me to a chair, and brought cool water, and washed the blood and sweat from me, as she had once before.

"Are you in much pain, Peter?"

"My head—only my head, Charmian. There is a bell ringing there—no—it is a hammer, beating."

And indeed I remembered little for a while, save the touch of her hands and the soothing murmur of her voice, until I found she was kneeling beside me, feeding me with broth from a spoon.

Wherefore I presently took the basin from her and emptied it at a gulp, and, finding myself greatly revived, made some effort to eat the supper she set before me.

Presently she came and sat beside me and ate also, watching me eat each morsel.

"Your poor hands!" she said; and looking down at them I saw that my knuckles were torn and broken, and the fingers were swollen.

"And yet," she went on, "except for the cut in your head, you are quite unmarked, Peter."

"He fought mostly for the body," I answered, "and I managed to keep my face out of the way."

When supper was finished she brought my pipe and filled it, and held the light for me. But my head throbbed woefully and for once the tobacco was flavourless; so I sighed and laid the pipe down.

"Why, Peter," Charmian said, regarding me with an anxious frown, "can't you smoke?"

"Not just now, Charmian," I answered.

Leaning my head in my hands, I fell into a sort of coma, until, feeling her touch upon my shoulder, I started and looked up.

"You must go to bed, Peter."

"No," I said.

"Yes, Peter."

"Very well, Charmian, yes—I will go to bed." And I rose.

"Do you feel better now, Peter?"

"Thank you, yes—much better."

"Then why do you hold on to the chair?"

"I am still a little giddy, but it will pass. And, Charmian—you forgive . . ."

"Yes, yes, and don't . . . don't look at me like that, Peter, and . . . oh, good-night . . . foolish boy!"

"I am twenty-five, Charmian!"

But as she turned away I saw that there were tears in her eyes.

A voice called my name very softly:

"Peter, oh, Peter, I want you. Oh, Peter... wake! Wake!"

I sat up in bed, and, as I listened, I grew suddenly sick and a fit of trembling shook me violently.

"Peter, oh, Peter, I am afraid! Wake... wake!"

I broke out in a cold sweat and glared helplessly towards the door.

"Quick, Peter ... come to me ... oh, God!"

I tried to move, but still I could not. And then, in the darkness, hands were shaking me wildly, and Charmian's voice was speaking in my ear.

"The door!" it whispered. "The door!"

Then I arose, and went into the outer room, with Charmian close beside me in the dark, and my eyes were upon the door. And then I saw a strange thing, for a thin line of white light traversed the floor from end to end.

Now, as I watched this narrow line, I saw that it was gradually widening and widening; very slowly, and with infinite emotion, the door was being opened from outside.

In this remote place, in this still, dead hour of the night, full of the ghostly hue that ever precedes the dawn, there was something devilish, something very like murder, in its stealthy motion.

I heard Charmian's breath catch, and in the

dark her hand came and crept into mine and her
fingers were as cold as death.

And then a great anger came upon me, and
I took a quick step forward, but Charmian re-
strained me.

"No, Peter!" she breathed. "Not yet ... wait!"
And she wound her arms round mine.

In a corner nearby stood that same trusty
staff that had been the companion of my wan-
derings, and so I reached and took it up, balanc-
ing it in my hand. And all the time I watched
that line of light upon the floor, widening and
widening, growing ever broader.

The minutes dragged slowly by, while the
line grew into a streak, and the streak into a
lane, and upon the lane came a blot that slowly
resolved itself into the shadow of a hand upon
the latch.

Slowly, slowly, to the hand came a wrist and
to the wrist an arm—another minute and this
maddening suspense would be over.

Despite Charmian's restraining clasp, I crept
a long pace nearer the softly moving door.

Thirty seconds more! I began to count; and,
gripping my staff, I braced myself for what might
be, when—with a sudden cry—Charmian sprang
forward, and, hurling herself against the door,
shut it with a crash.

"Quick, Peter!" She panted. I was beside her
almost as she spoke, and had my hand upon the
latch.

"I must see who this was," I said.

"You are mad!" she cried.

"Let me open the door, Charmian."

"No, no . . . I say, no!"

"Whoever it was must not escape. Open the door!"

"Never, never . . . I tell you . . . death is outside, there's murder in the very air, I feel it . . . and . . . dear God . . . the door has no bolt."

"They are gone now, whoever they were," I said reassuringly. "The danger is over—if danger it could be called."

"Danger!" cried Charmian. "I tell you—it was death."

"Yet, after all, it may have been only some homeless wanderer."

"Then why that deadly, silent caution?"

"True!" I said, becoming thoughtful.

"Bring the table, Peter, and set it across the door."

"Surely the table is too light to . . ."

"But it will give sufficient warning, not that I shall sleep again tonight. Oh, Peter! Had I not been dreaming and happened to wake . . . had I not chanced to look towards the door, it would have opened . . . wide, and then . . . oh, horrible!"

"You were dreaming?"

"A hateful, hateful dream, and awoke in terror, and, being afraid, I glanced towards the door and saw it opening . . . and now . . . bring the table, Peter."

Now, groping about, my hand encountered one of the candles, and taking out my tinder-box I lit it.

Charmian was leaning against the door, clad in a flowing white garment, a garment that was wonderfully stitched, all dainty frills and laces, with here and there a bow of blue ribbon.

And up from this foam of laces her shoulders rose, white and soft, and dimpled, sweeping up in noble lines to the smooth round column of her throat.

But as I stared at all this loveliness she gave a sudden gasp, and stooped her head, and crossed her hands upon her bosom, while up over the snow of shoulder, over neck, cheek, and brow, ebbed that warm crimson tide.

I could only gaze and gaze, till, with a swift movement, she crossed to that betraying candle and, stooping, blew out the light.

Then I set the table across the door, having done which I stood looking towards where she still stood.

"Charmian," I said.

"Yes, Peter."

"Tomorrow . . ."

"Yes, Peter?"

"I will make a bar to hold the door."

"Yes, Peter."

"Two bars would be better, perhaps?"

"Yes, Peter."

"You would feel safe then?"

"Safer than ever, Peter."

135

* * *

Some days after this, while walking up the road to the Hollow, I happened to meet up once again with the talkative peddler.

Engaging me again in conversation, rather against my will, he brought up the subject of my cottage in the Hollow.

"Ah, indeed! I came through this very afternoon, and uncommon pretty everything was looking, with the grass so green and the trees so—so . . ."

"Shady."

"Shady's the word!" The peddler nodded, glancing up at me through his narrowed eyelids, and chuckled. "A paradise you might call it—ah! A paradise or a—Garden of Eden, with Eve and the serpent and all!"

He broke out into a cackling laugh.

"Yes?"

"You see, I happened to pass the cottage— and very pretty that looked too, and nice and neat inside. And, being so near, I happened to glance in at the window, and there, sure enough, I see—her—as you might say, Eve.

"Well, just as I happened to look in at the window, she happened to be standing with an open book in her hand—an old, leather book with a broken cover."

"Yes?"

"And she was laughing—and a pretty, soft Eve's laugh it were too."

"Yes?"

"And he was looking at the book—over her shoulder!"

The irons slipped from my grasp and fell with a harsh clang.

"I says to you—I says—look out! A fine, handsome lass she be, with her soft eyes and red lips, and long, white arms—the eyes, lips, and arms of an Eve; and Eve tricked Adam, didn't she? And you ain't a better man than Adam, are you? Very well, then!"

Then he spat into the ditch and, shouldering his pack, strode away.

And, after some while, I trudged on towards the cottage. As I went I repeated to myself, over and over again, the word "liar."

Yet my step was very slow and heavy, and my feet dragged in the dust; and somewhere in my head a small hammer had begun to beat softly, slow and regular, but beating, beating upon my brain.

For the upper cover of my Virgil book was broken!

* * *

A man was leaning in the shadow of a tree, looking down into the Hollow.

I could not see him very distinctly because,

though evening had scarcely fallen, the shadows where he stood were very dense, but he was gazing down into the Hollow in the attitude of one who waits. For what? For whom?

Very cautiously I began creeping nearer the passive figure, a shortish, broad-shouldered figure, clad in a blue coat. He held his hat in his hand, and he leaned carelessly against the tree, and his easy assurance of air maddened me the more.

A stick snapped sharp and loud beneath my foot, the lounging back stiffened and grew rigid, the face showed for an instant over the shoulder and with a spring, he had vanished into the bushes.

It was a vain hope to find a man in such a dense tangle of boughs and underbrush; though I sought eagerly upon all sides he had made good his escape.

So, after a while, I retraced my steps, turning aside to that precipitous path which leads down into the Hollow.

Now as I went, listening to the throb of the hammer in my head, whom should I meet but Charmian, coming gaily through the green, and singing as she came.

At the sight of me she stopped and the song died upon her lips.

"Why, why, Peter . . . you look dreadfully pale. . . ."

"Thank you, I am very well!"

"You have not been fighting again?"

"Why should I have been fighting, Charmian?"

"Your eyes are wild ... and fierce, Peter."

"Were you coming to—to—meet me, Charmian?"

"Yes, Peter."

Now watching beneath my brows, it almost seemed that her colour had changed and that her eyes avoided mine. Could it be that she was equivocating?

"But I am much before my usual time, to-night, Charmian."

"Then there will be no waiting for supper, and I am ravenous, Peter!"

And as she led the way along the path she began to sing again.

On reaching the cottage I set down the iron bars I was carrying with a clang.

"These are the bars I promised to make for the door."

"Do you always keep your promises, Peter?"

"I hope so."

"Then if you promise me always to come home by the road, and never through the coppice ... you will do so, won't you?"

"Why should I?"

"Because the coppice is so dark and lonely, and if ... I say, if I should take it into my head to come and meet you sometimes, there would be no chance of my missing you."

And so she looked at me and smiled, and

going back to her cooking she started singing again while I sat and watched her beneath my brows.

Surely, surely no woman whose heart was full of deceit could sing so blithely and happily, or look at one with such sweet candour in her eyes?

And yet the supper was a very ghost of a meal, for when I remembered the man who had watched and waited, the food seemed to choke me.

'She's an Eve—an Eve!' rang a voice in my ear. 'Eve tricked Adam, didn't she, and you ain't a better man than Adam. She's an Eve—an Eve!'

"Charmian," I said at last.

"Yes, Peter?"

"Do you—ever see any—any men lurking about the Hollow when I am away?"

Her needle stopped suddenly, and she did not look up as she answered:

"No, Peter."

"Never? Are you sure, Charmian?"

The needle began to fly to and fro again, but still she did not look up.

"No, of course not, how should I see anyone? I scarcely go beyond the Hollow, and . . . I'm busy all day."

'An Eve—an Eve!' said a voice in my ear. 'Eve tricked Adam, didn't she? An Eve!'

After this I sat for a long time without moving, my mind harassed with doubts and a hideous, morbid dread. Why had she avoided my eye? Her own were pure and truthful, and could not lie!

Why, why had they avoided mine? If only she had looked at me!

Presently I rose, and began to pace up and down the room.

"You are very restless, Peter!"

"Indeed, I had not thought of my books."

"Then read me something aloud, Peter."

"I will read you the sorrow of Achilles for the loss of Briseis," I answered.

And going into the corner, I raised my hand to my shelf of books and stood there with hand upraised yet touching no book, for a sudden spasm seemed to have me in its clutches.

Once again the trembling seized me, and the hammer had recommenced its beat, beating upon my brain.

And in a while, I turned from my books and crossing to the door leaned there with my back to her, lest she should see my face just then.

"I—I don't think I will read tonight!" I said at last.

"Very well, Peter, let us talk."

"Or talk," I said. "I—I think I'll go to bed. Please excuse me—I'm very tired."

So, while she still stared at me, I turned

away and, mumbling a good-night, went into my room, and closing the door leaned against it, for my mind was sick with dread and sorrow, and a great anguish.

For now I knew that Charmian had lied to me—my Virgil book had been moved from its usual place.

* * *

The next morning I arose early, unable to sleep, and set out, with my mind in a turmoil, for the brook, where I was used to taking my morning wash.

"Tomorrow," I said, clenching my fists, "tomorrow I will go away."

I turned aside to the brook, and, kneeling down, I gazed at myself in the dark, still water; and I saw that the night had indeed set its mark upon me.

"Tomorrow," I said again, nodding to the wild face below, "tomorrow I will go far away."

Now while I gazed at myself I heard a sudden gasp behind me, and turning saw Charmian.

"Peter! Is it you?" she whispered, drawing back from me.

"Who else, Charmian? Did I startle you?"

"Yes . . . oh, Peter!"

"Are you afraid of me?"

"You are like one who has walked with . . . death!"

I rose to my feet and stood looking down at her.

"Are you afraid of me, Charmian?"

"No, Peter."

"I am glad of that," I said, "because I want to ask you to marry me, Charmian."

Chapter
Six

"Peter!"

"Yes?"

"I wish you wouldn't."

"Wouldn't what, Charmian?"

"Stir your tea round, and round, and round —it is really most—exasperating!"

"I beg your pardon!" I said humbly.

"And you eat nothing, and that is also exasperating."

"I am not hungry."

"And I was so careful with the bacon—see, it is fried, beautifully, yes—you are very exasperating, Peter!"

Here, finding I was absent-mindedly stirring my tea round and round again, I gulped it down out of the way, whereupon Charmian took my cup and refilled it, having done which, she set her elbows upon the table, and, propping her chin in her hands, looked at me.

"You climbed out through your window last night, Peter?"

"Yes."

"It must have been a dreadfully tight squeeze!"

"Yes."

"And why did you go by the window?"

"I did not wish to disturb you."

"That was very thoughtful of you, only, you see, I was up and dressed; the roar of the thunder woke me. It was a dreadful storm, Peter."

"Yes."

"The lightning was awful!"

"Yes."

"And you were out in it?"

"Yes."

"Oh, you poor, poor Peter! How cold you must have been."

"On the contrary," I began, "I . . ."

"And wet, Peter, miserably wet and clammy!"

"I did not notice it," I murmured.

"Being a philosopher, Peter, and too much engrossed in your thoughts?"

"I was certainly thinking."

"Of yourself!"

"Yes . . ."

"You are a great egoist, aren't you, Peter?"

"Am I, Charmian?"

"Who but an egoist could stand with his mind so full of himself and his own concerns as to be oblivious to thunder and lightning, and not know that he is miserably clammy and wet?"

"I thought of others besides myself."

"But only in connection with yourself; everything you have ever read, or seen, you apply to yourself, to make that self more worthy in Mr. Vibart's eyes. Is this worthy of Peter Vibart?

"Can Peter Vibart do this, that, or the other, and still retain the respect of Peter Vibart? Then why, being in all things so very correct and precise, why is Peter Vibart given to prowling abroad at midnight, quite oblivious to thunder, lightning, wet, and clamminess?

"I answer: Because Peter Vibart is too much engrossed by . . . Peter Vibart. There! That sounds rather cryptic, and very full of Peter Vibart, but that is as it should be." She laughed.

"And what does it mean, Charmian?"

"Good Sir, the Sibyl hath spoken! Find her meaning for yourself."

"You have called me, on various occasions, a 'creature' a 'pedant,' very frequently a pedant, and now it seems I am an egoist, and all because . . ."

"Because you think too much, Peter; you never open your lips without having first thought out just what you are going to say; you never do anything without having laboriously mapped it all out beforehand, that you may not outrage

146

Peter Vibart's tranquillity by any impulsive act or speech.

"Oh! You are always thinking and thinking, and that is even worse than stirring and stirring at your tea, as you are doing now."

I took the spoon hastily from my cup, and laid it as far out of reach as possible.

"If ever you should write the book you once spoke of, it would be just the very sort of book that I should . . . hate."

"Why, Charmian?"

"Because it would be a book of artfully turned phrases, a book in which all the characters, especially women, would think and speak, and act by rote and rule . . . as according to Mr. Peter Vibart.

"It would be a scholarly book, of elaborate finish and care of detail, with no irregularities of style, or anything else, to break the monotonous harmony of the whole . . . indeed, Sir, it would be a most unreadable book!"

"Do you think so, Charmian?" I answered, once more taking up the teaspoon.

"Why, of course!" she answered, with raised brows. "It would probably be full of Greek and Latin quotations! And you would polish and re-write it until you had polished every vestige of life and spontaneity out of it, as you do out of yourself, with your thinking, your endless thinking."

"But I never quote you Greek or Latin—that

is surely something, and, as for thinking, would you have me a thoughtless fool or an impulsive ass?"

"Anything rather than a calculating, introspective philosopher, seeing only the mote in the sunbeam, and nothing of the glory."

Here she gently disengaged the teaspoon from my fingers, and laid it in her own saucer, having done which, she sighed, and looked at me with her head to one side.

"Were they all like you, Peter, I wonder ... those old philosophers, grim and stern, and terribly repressed, with burning eyes, Peter, and with very long chins? Epictetus was, of course!"

"And you dislike Epictetus, Charmian?"

"I detest him! He was just the kind of person, Peter, who, being unable to sleep, would have wandered out into a terrible thunderstorm, in the middle of the night, and being cold and wet and clammy, Peter, would have drawn moral lessons, and made epigrams upon the thunder and lightning. Epictetus, I am quite sure, was a ... person!"

"He was one of the wisest, gentlest, and most lovable of all the Stoics!" I answered.

"Can a philosopher possibly be lovable, Peter?"

Here I very absent-mindedly took up a fork, but, finding her eyes upon me, laid it down again.

"You are very nervous, Peter, and very pale, and worn, and haggard, and all because you

148

habitually overthink yourself; and indeed, there is something very far wrong with a man who perseveringly stirs an empty cup ... with a fork!"

And with a laugh she took my cup, and having once more refilled it she set it before me.

"And yet, Peter, I don't think—no, I don't think I would have you very much changed, after all."

"You mean that you would rather I remained the pedantic, egotistical creature ..."

"I mean, Peter, that, being a woman, I naturally love novelty, and you are very novel and very interesting."

"Thank you!" I replied, frowning.

"And more contradictory than any woman!"

"Hum!"

"You are so strong and simple, so wise and brave, and so very weak, and foolish, and timid!"

"Timid?" I asked.

"Timid!" She nodded.

"I am a vast fool!" I acknowledged.

"And I never knew a man anything like you before, Peter!"

"And you have known many, I understand?"

"Very many."

"Yes, you told me so once before, I believe."

"Twice, Peter; and each time you became very silent and gloomy! Now you, on the other hand," she continued, "have known very few women?"

"And my life has been calm and unruffled in consequence!"

"You had your books, Peter, and your horse-shoes."

"My books and horseshoes, yes."

"And were content?"

"Quite content."

"Until, one day a woman came to you."

"Until one day I met a woman."

"And then . . ."

"And then—I asked her to marry me, Charmian."

Here there ensued a pause during which Charmian began to pleat a fold in the tablecloth.

"That was rather . . . unwise of you, wasn't it?" she answered at last.

"How unwise?"

"Because . . . she might . . . have taken you at your word, Peter."

"Do you mean that—that you won't, Charmian?"

"Oh dear, no! I have arrived at no decision yet . . . how could I? You must give me time to consider."

Here she paused in her pleating to regard it critically, with her head on one side.

"To be sure, you need someone to . . . to look after you . . . that is very evident!"

"Yes."

"To cook . . . and to wash for you."

"Yes."

"To mend your clothes for you."

"Yes."

"And you think me sufficiently ... competent?"

"Oh, Charmian, I—yes."

"Thank you!" she said, very solemnly.

Though her lashes had drooped I felt the mockery of her eyes, so I took a sudden great gulp of tea and came near to choking, while Charmian began to pleat another fold in the tablecloth.

"And so Mr. Vibart would stoop to wed so humble a person as Charmian Brown? Mr. Peter Vibart would actually marry a woman of whose past he knows nothing?"

"Yes."

"That again would be rather ... unwise, wouldn't it?"

"Why?"

"Considering Mr. Vibart's very lofty ideals in regard to women."

"What do you mean?"

"Didn't you once say that your wife's name must be above suspicion?"

"Did I? Yes, perhaps I did—well?"

"Well, this woman ... this Humble Person, has no name at all and no shred of reputation left to her. She has compromised herself beyond all redemption in the eyes of the world.

"But then, this world and I have always mutually despised each other."

"She ran away, this woman ... eloped with

151

the most notorious, most accomplished Rake in London."

"Well?"

"Oh, is that not enough?"

"Enough for what, Charmian?"

I saw her busy fingers falter and tremble, but her voice was steady when she answered:

"Enough to make any wise man think twice before asking this Humble Person to ... to marry him."

"I might think twenty times, and it would be all one!"

"You mean ... ?"

"That if Charmian Brown will stoop to marry a village blacksmith, Peter Vibart will find happiness again. A happiness that is not of the sunshine, nor the wind in the trees. Lord, what a fool I was!"

Her fingers had stopped altogether now, but she neither spoke nor raised her head.

"Charmian," I said, leaning nearer across the table, "please speak."

"Oh, Peter!" she said, with a sudden break in her voice, and bent her head lower.

Yet in a little while she looked up at me, and her eyes were very sweet and shining.

Now, as our eyes met, up from throat to brow there crept that hot, slow wave of colour, and in her face and in her eyes I seemed to read joy, fear, shame, and radiant joy again.

But then she bent her head once more, and I grew suddenly afraid of her and of myself, and longed to hurl aside the table that divided us.

Instead I thrust my hands deep into my pockets, and finding there my tobacco pipe, brought it out and turned it aimlessly over and over.

I would have spoken, only I knew that my voice would tremble, and so I sat silently staring at my pipe with unseeing eyes, and with my brain in a ferment.

And presently came her voice, cool, sweet, and sane:

"Your tobacco, Peter." And she held the box towards me across the table.

"Ah, thank you!" I said, and began to fill my pipe, while she watched me with her chin propped in her hands.

"Peter!"

"Yes, Charmian?"

"I wonder why so grave a person as Mr. Peter Vibart should seek to marry so impossible a creature as . . . the Humble Person?"

"I think," I answered, "I think, if there is any special reason, it is because of your mouth."

"My mouth?"

"Or your eyes—or the way you have with your lashes."

Charmian laughed, and instantly drooped them at me, and laughed again, and shook her head.

153

"But surely, Peter, surely there are thousands, millions, of women with mouths and eyes like ... the Humble Person's?"

"It is possible;" I said, "but none who have the same way with their lashes."

"What do you mean?"

"I can't tell. I don't know."

"Don't you, Peter?"

"No, it is just a way."

"And so it is that you want to marry this very Humble Person?"

"I think I have wanted to from the very first, but did not know it—being a blind fool!"

"And ... did it need a night walk in a thunerstorm to teach you?"

"No, that is, yes—perhaps it did."

"And, are you quite, quite sure?"

"Quite, quite sure!" I said.

As I spoke I laid my pipe upon the table and rose; and because my hands were trembling I clenched my fists.

But as I approached her, she started up and put out a hand to hold me off, and then I saw that her hands were trembling also.

Standing thus, she spoke very softly:

"Peter."

"Yes, Charmian?"

"Do you remember describing to me the ... the perfect woman who should be your ... wife?"

"Yes."

"How you must be able to respect her for her intellect?"

"Yes."

"Honour her for her virtue?"

"Yes, Charmian."

"And worship her for her . . . spotless purity?"

"I dreamed a paragon, perfect and impossible; I was a fool!" I said.

"Impossible! Oh, Peter! What . . . what do you mean?"

"She was only an impalpable shade quite impossible of realisation, a bloodless thing, as you said, and quite unnatural, a sickly figment of the imagination—I was a fool!"

"And you are . . . too wise now to expect . . . such virtues in any woman?"

"Yes," I said. "No—oh, Charmian! I only know that you have taken this phantom's place, that you fill all my thoughts, sleeping and waking. . . ."

"No! No!" she cried, and struggled in my arms, so that I caught her hands, and held them close, and kissed them many times.

"Oh, Charmian! Charmian! Don't you know —can't you see—it is you I want—you, and only you, forever. Whatever you were, whatever you are, I love you—love you and always will! Marry me, Charmian—marry me! And you shall be dearer than my life—more to me than my soul. . . ."

But as I spoke, her hands were snatched

away, her eyes blazed into mine, and her lips were all bitter scorn; and, seeing this, Fear came upon me.

"Marry you!" She panted. "Marry you? No ...no...no!"

So she stamped her foot and sobbed, and, turning, fled from me, out of the cottage.

And now to Fear came Wonder, and with Wonder was Despair.

Truly, was ever man so great a fool!

*　　*　　*

The next morning I was at the smithy early. But upon the threshold I stopped all at once, and drew softly back.

Despite the early hour, Prudence was there, upon her knees before the anvil, with George's great hand-hammer clasped to her bosom, sobbing over it, and while she sobbed, she kissed its worn handle.

And because such love was sacred and hallowed that dingy place, I took off my hat as I once more crossed the road.

Seeing the Bull was not yet open, for the day was still young, I sat down in the porch and sighed.

And after I had sat there for some while, plunged in bitter meditation, I became aware of the door opening, and the next moment a tremulous hand was laid upon my head, and, looking round, I saw the Ancient.

"And now, Peter," the old man said, "now for the news—about Black Jarge."

"What of him, Ancient?"

"It took eight of them to do it, Peter, and now four of them's laying in their beds, and four of them's hobbling on crutches, and all over a couple of rabbits."

"Do you mean that George has been taken a prisoner?"

The Ancient nodded, and inhaled his pinch of snuff with evident relish.

"What have they done with him? Where is he, Ancient?"

But before the old man could answer, Simon and Joe appeared.

"Ah, Peter!" Simon said, shaking his head. "The Gaffer's been telling you how they've taken Jarge for poaching, I suppose. . . ."

"Well, he won't never do it no more," Job said. "What with poaching game and knocking keepers about, it isn't very likely that Squire Beverley will let him off very easy. . . ."

"Who?" I said, looking up, and speaking for the first time.

"Squire Beverley of Burnham Hall."

"Sir Peregrine Beverley?"

"Ay, for sure."

"And how far is it to Burnham Hall?"

"It be a matter of eight miles, Peter," the Ancient answered.

"Then I had better start now."

"Why, Peter, where are you going?"

"To Burnham Hall, Ancient."

"Then, by the Lord, I'll go with you."

"It's a long walk!"

"No, Simon shall drive us in the cart."

"That I will!" nodded the Innkeeper.

"Ay, lad," cried the Ancient, laying his hand upon my arm, "we'll go and see the Squire, you and me—shall us, Peter? Black Jarge isn't a convict yet, let fools say what they will; we'll show them, Peter, we'll show them!"

So saying, the old man led me into the kitchen of the Bull, while Simon went to harness the horses.

A cheery place at all times is the kitchen of an English Inn, a comfortable place to eat in, to talk in, or to doze in.

And what Inn kitchen in all England was ever brighter, neater, and more comfortable than this kitchen of the Bull, where sweet Prue held supreme sway.

But today Prue's eyes were red, and her lips were all drooping, which, though her smile was brave and ready, the Ancient was quick to notice.

"Why, Prue, lass, you've been weeping!"

"Oh! It's nothing, dear, it's just a maid's foolishness, never mind me."

"Ah! But I love you, Prue—come, kiss me—there now, tell me all about it—all about it, Prue."

"Oh, Grandfather!" she said from the hollow of his shoulder, "it's just . . . Jarge!"

"Did you, did you say Jarge, Prue? Is it breaking your heart you be for that there poaching Black Jarge?"

Prudence slipped from his encircling arm and stood up very straight and proud; there were tears thick upon her lashes, but she did not attempt to wipe them away.

"Grandfather, you mustn't speak of Jarge to me like that . . . you mustn't because I . . . love him, and if he ever comes back I'll marry him if . . . if he will only ask me; and if he never comes back, then I think I shall . . . die!"

The Ancient took out his snuff-box, knocked it, opened it, glanced inside, and shut it up again.

"Wishful to wed him she is, and so she shall. Kiss me again, Prue, for I am going to see Squire —ay, I am going to go and speak with Squire for Jarge—and Peter is coming too."

"Oh, Mr. Peter! Is this true?"

"Yes."

"Do you think the Squire will see you . . . listen to you?"

"I think he will, Prudence."

"Last time you met with Jarge, he tried to kill you. Oh, I know, and now . . . you are going to . . ."

"Nonsense, Prue!" I said.

159

But as I spoke she stooped, and would have kissed my hand, but I raised her and kissed her upon the cheek instead.

"For good luck, Prue," I said, and so turned and left her.

The last thing I saw was the light in Prue's sweet eyes as she watched us from the open lattice.

Riding along in the cart, we had not gone above a mile or so from the village when we were suddenly surprised by a man darting across the road ahead of us. He vanished almost immediately into the trees, but there was no mistaking that broad-shouldered figure, it was Black George himself.

Seeing, therefore, no further purpose in our mission, we turned the cart round, and the other two jogged back to the village, while I turned aside towards the Hollow.

It was with some little trepidation that I descended into the Hollow, and walked along beside the brook, for soon I should meet Charmian. And the memory of our parting, and the thought of this meeting, had been in my mind all day long.

She would not be expecting me yet, for I was much before my usual time, so I walked on slowly beside the brook, deliberating on what I should say to her, until I came to that large stone where I had sat dreaming the night when she had stood in the moonlight and first called me in to supper.

Now, sinking upon this stone, I fell into a profound meditation.

From this I was suddenly aroused by the clink of iron and the snort of a horse.

Wondering, I lifted my eyes, but the bushes were very dense and I could see nothing. But in a little, borne upon the gentle wind, came the sound of a voice, low and soft and very sweet, whose rich tones there was no mistaking, followed, almost immediately, by another, deeper, gruffer—the voice of a man.

With a bound I was upon my feet, and somehow I crossed the brook, but even so, I was too late. There was the crack of a whip, followed by the muffled thud of a horse's hoofs, which died quickly away and was lost in the stir of leaves.

I ground my teeth and cursed that fate which seemed determined that I should not meet this man face to face, this man whose back I had seen but once—a broad-shouldered back clad in a blue coat.

I stood where I was, dumb and rigid.

She was approaching by that leafy path that wound its way along beside the brook, and there came upon me a physical nausea, and the thud of the hammer grew more maddening.

Suddenly the trees and bushes swung giddily round, the grass swayed beneath my feet, and Charmian was beside me, with her arm about my shoulders; but I pushed her from me, and leaned against a tree nearby.

"Please, Charmian, do not touch me again; it is too soon after . . ."

"What do you mean . . . Peter? What do you mean?"

"He has—been with you—again. . . ."

"What do you mean?" she cried.

"I know of his visits—if he was the same as last time—in a blue coat—no, don't, don't touch me!"

But she had sprung upon me, and caught me by the arms, and shook me in a grip so strong that, giddy as I was, I reeled and staggered like a drunken man. And still her voice hissed:

"What do you mean?"

"I mean that you are a Messalina, a Julia, a Joan of Naples, as beautiful as they—and as wanton."

Now at the word she cried out, and struck me twice across the face, blows that burnt and stung.

"Liar! Oh, you poor, blind, self-deluding fool! I shall always remember you as I see you now . . . scarlet-cheeked, shame-faced . . . a beaten hound!"

And, speaking, she shook her hand at me and turned upon her heel; but in that instant I clasped my arms about her, and caught her up, and crushed her close and high against my breast.

"Go," I said. "Go—no—no—not yet!"

And then she struggled to break my clasp, fiercely, desperately; her long hair burst its fastenings and enveloped us both in its rippling splendour.

She beat my face, she wound her fingers in my hair, but my lips smiled on, for the hammer in my brain had deadened all else.

And presently she lay still. I felt her body relax and grow suddenly pliable and soft; her head fell back across my arm, and as she lay I saw the tears of her helplessness ooze out beneath her drooping lashes.

So, with her long hair trailing over me, I carried her to the cottage. Closing the door behind me with my foot, I crossed the room and set her down upon the bed.

"Why did you lie to me, Charmian? Why did you lie to me? I asked you once if you ever saw men hereabouts when I was away, do you remember? You told me no, and while you spoke I knew you lied, for I had seen him standing among the leaves, waiting and watching for you.

"I once asked you if you were ever lonely when I was away, and you answered 'no, you were too busy, seldom went beyond the Hollow,' do you remember? And yet you had brought him here—here, into the cottage—he had looked at my Virgil, over your shoulder, do you remember?"

"You were spying!"

"You know I did not; had I seen him I should have killed him, because I loved you. I loved you with every breath I drew. I think I must have shown you something of this, from time to time, for you are very clever, and you must have laughed over it together—you and he.

"Can you imagine, I wonder, the agony of it, the haunting horrors of imagination, the bitter days, the sleepless nights? To see you so beautiful, so glorious, and know you so base!"

Now she strove no more against me, only in her face was bitter scorn, and an anger that cast out fear.

"I hate you . . . despise you!" she whispered. "I hate you more than any man was ever hated!"

Inch by inch I drew her to me, until she stood close, within the circle of my arms.

"And I think I love you more than any woman was ever loved! For the glorious beauty of your strong, sweet body, for the temptation of your eyes, for the red lure of your lips!"

I stopped and kissed her full upon the mouth. She lay soft and warm in my embrace, all unresisting, only she shivered beneath my kiss, and a great sob rent her bosom.

"And I also think that, because of the perfidity of your heart, I hate you as much as you do me—as much as ever woman, dead or living, was hated by man, and shall be forever!"

While I spoke I let her go, and, turning, I strode swiftly out and away from the cottage.

I hurried on, looking neither to right nor left, seeing only the face of Charmian, fearful and appealing, then blazing with scorn.

And here, where the shadow was deepest, I came upon a lurking figure—a figure I recognised, a figure there was no mistaking, and which I should have known anywhere.

A shortish, broad-shouldered man, clad in a blue coat, who stood with his back towards me, looking down into the Hollow, in the attitude of one who waits.

He was cut off from me by a solitary bush. I cleared this bush at a bound, and before the fellow had realised my presence, I had pinned him by the collar.

"Damn you! Show your face!" I cried, and swung him round so fiercely that he staggered, and his hat fell off.

Then as I saw, I clasped my head between my hands, and fell back, staring.

A grizzled man with an honest, open face, a middle-aged man whose homely features were lighted by a pair of kindly blue eyes, just now round with astonishment.

"Lord—Mr. Peter!" he exclaimed.

"Adam! Oh, God forgive me, it's Adam!"

I stared at my old groom in surprise.

"Tell me—quick!" I said, catching his hand in mine. "You have been here many times before of late?"

"Why, yes, Mr. Peter, but . . ."

"Quick!" I said. "On one occasion she took you into the cottage yonder and showed you a book—you looked at it over her shoulder?"

"Yes, Sir—but . . ."

"What sort of book was it?"

"An old book, Sir, with the cover broken and with your name written on the inside of it—it was that way as she found out who you were. . . ."

"Oh, Adam! Oh, Adam! Now may God help me!"

And, dropping his hand, I turned and ran until I reached the cottage; but it was empty; Charmian had gone.

And now the full knowledge of my madness rushed upon me in an overwhelming flood; but with Misery was a great and mighty Joy, for now I knew her worthy of all respect and honour and worship, for her intellect, for her proud virtue, and for her spotless purity.

So thus with Joy came Remorse and abiding Sorrow.

Then gradually my arms crept about the pillow where her head had so often rested, and I kissed it, laid my head upon it and sighed, and so fell into a troubled sleep.

* * *

The chill of dawn was in the air when I awoke, and it was some few moments before, with a rush, I remembered why I was kneeling there beside Charmian's bed.

I could not bear to stay longer in the cottage, and, thinking I might lose my misery in hard work, I set off towards the village and the forge.

Drawing near to the Bull, I saw a figure standing in the early sunlight; a wild figure in the dawn, with matted hair and beard, and clad in tattered clothes; yet hair and beard gleamed a reddish gold where the light touched them, and there was but one man I knew so tall and so mighty as this.

"George!" I said, and held out my hand. He turned swiftly, but, seeing me, stepped back a pace, staring.

"Peter?" he said at last, speaking hardly above a whisper. "But you're dead, Peter, dead—I killed you. You see, I tried so hard to kill you, so cruel hard, Peter, and I thought I had.

"I thought that was why they took me, and so I broke my way out of the lock-up, to come and say good-bye to Prue's window, and then I was going back to give myself up and let them hang me if they wanted to."

"Were you, George?"

"Yes."

Here George turned to look at me, and looking, dropped his eyes and fumbled with his hands, while up under his tanned skin there crept a painful, burning crimson.

"Peter!" he said.

"It's likely you've been thinking me a poor

sort of man after what—what I just told you. A coward?"

"I think you more of a man than ever."

"Why then, Peter, if you do think that, here's my hand, if you'll take it, and I bid you good-bye!"

"I'll take your hand, and gladly, George, but not to wish you good-bye—it shall be, rather, to bid you welcome home again."

"No," he cried. "No, I couldn't—I couldn't bear to see you and Prue married, Peter—no, I couldn't bear it."

"And you never will, George. Prue loves a stronger, better man than I. She has wept over him, George, and prayed over him, such tears and prayers as surely might win the blackest soul to Heaven, and has said that she would marry the man.

"Yes, George, even if he came back with fetter-marks upon him, even then she would marry him—if he would only ask her."

"Oh, Peter!" George cried, seizing my shoulders in a mighty grip and looking into my eyes, with tears in his own.

"It is God's truth. And look, there is a sign to prove I am no liar—look!"

George turned, and I felt his fingers tighten suddenly, for there at the open doorway of the Inn, with the early glory of the morning all about her, stood Prue. As we watched, she began to cross the road towards the smithy, with laggard step and drooping head.

"Do you know where she is going, George? I can tell you, she is going to your smith, to pray for you—do you hear, to pray for you! Come!"

"No, Peter, no! I dare not—I couldn't."

But he let me lead him forward nevertheless.

And behold! Prue was kneeling before the anvil, with her face hidden in her arms, and her slender body swaying slightly. But all at once, as if she felt him near her, she raised her head and saw him, then sprang to her feet with a glad cry.

And, as she stood, George went to her and knelt at her feet; then, raising the hem of her gown, he stooped and kissed it.

"Oh, my sweet maid! Oh, my sweet Prue! I am not worthy, I am not . . ."

But she caught the great shaggy head to her bosom and stifled it there.

And in her face was a radiance, a happiness beyond words, and the man's strong arms clung close about her.

So I turned, and left them in paradise together.

Chapter
Seven

One day about a week later, as I sat alone in the smithy, I became conscious of a very delicate perfume in the air, and also that someone had entered quietly. I did not at once look up, fearing to dispel the hope that tingled within me.

So I remained with my face still covered, until something touched me, and I saw that it was the gold-mounted handle of a whip, wherefore I raised my head suddenly and glanced up.

Then I saw a radiant vision in polished riding-boots and speckless moleskins, in handsome flowered waistcoat and perfect-fitting coat, with snowy frills at throat and wrists.

A tall, gallant figure, with a graceful insolence, tapping his boot lightly with his whip.

But, as his eyes met mine, his languid expression vanished, he came a quick step nearer, and bent his face nearer my own, a dark face, handsome in its way, pale and aquiline, with a powerful jaw and dominating eyes and mouth.

Now, glancing up at his brow, I saw there a small, newly healed scar.

"Is it possible?" he said, speaking in that softly modulated voice I remembered having heard once before. "Can it be possible that I address my worthy cousin? That shirt! That utterly impossible coat! And yet, the likeness is remarkable! Have I the honour to address Mr. Peter Vibart—late of Oxford?"

"The same, Sir."

"'Pon my soul!" he said, eyeing me languidly through his glass again. "'Pon my soul! You are damnably like me, you know, in features."

"Damnably!"

He glanced at me sharply, and laughed.

"It is a strange thing," he continued, as he dusted his fingers on his handkerchief, "a very strange thing that, being cousins, we have never met till now—especially as I have heard so very much about you."

"But we have met before, and the circumstances were then even more dramatic, perhaps; we met in a tempest, Sir."

"Ha!" he exclaimed, dwelling on the word, and speaking very slowly. "A tempest, cousin?"

"There was much wind and rain, and it was very dark."

"Dark, cousin?"

"But I saw your face very plainly as you lay

171

on your back, Sir, by the aid of a postillion's lanthorn, and was greatly struck by our mutual resemblance."

Sir Maurice raised his glass and looked at me, and as he looked, he smiled, but he could not hide the sudden, passionate quiver of his thin nostrils, or the gleam of his eyes beneath their languid lids.

He rose slowly and paced to the door; when he came back again he was laughing softly.

"So, it was you?" he murmured, with a pause between the words. "Oh, was ever anything so damnably contrary! To think that I should hunt her into your very arms!"

He laughed again, but, as he did so, the stout riding-whip snapped in his hands like a straw. He glanced down at the broken pieces, and from them to me.

"You see, I am rather strong in the hands, cousin, but I was not quite strong enough last time we met, though, to be sure, as you say, it was very dark. Had I known it was worthy Cousin Peter's throat I grasped, I think I might have squeezed it just a little tighter."

"Sir, I really don't think you could have done so."

"Yes." He sighed, tossing his broken whip into a corner. "Yes, I think so—you see, I mistook you for merely an interfering country bumpkin...."

"Yes, while I, on the other hand, took you for a fine gentleman nobly intent on the ruin of

172

an unfortunate, friendless girl, whose poverty would seem to make her an easy victim. . . ."

"In which it appears you were as much mistaken as I, Cousin Peter."

"Indeed?"

"Why, surely—surely you must know. Did she tell you nothing of herself?"

"Very little besides her name."

"Ah! She told you her name, then?"

"Yes, she told me her name."

"Well, cousin?"

"Well, Sir?"

We had both risen, and now fronted each other across the anvil, Sir Maurice debonaire and smiling, while I stood frowning and gloomy.

"Come," I said at last, "let us understand each other once and for all. I tell you I never was your rival in the past, and never shall be in the future."

"Meaning, cousin?"

"Meaning, Sir, in regard to either the legacy or the Lady Sophia Sefton. I was never fond enough of money to marry for it. I have never seen this lady, nor do I propose to; thus, so far as I am concerned, you are free to win her and the fortune as soon as you will.

"I, as you see, prefer horseshoes."

"And what," said Sir Maurice, flicking a speck of soot from his cuff, and immediately looking at me again, "what of Charmian?"

"I don't know, nor should I be likely to tell

you if I did. Wherever she may be, she is safe, I trust, and beyond your reach. . . ."

"No, she will never be beyond my reach until she is dead, or I am—perhaps not even then. And I shall find her again, sooner or later, depend upon it—yes, you may depend upon that!"

"Cousin Maurice, wherever she may be, she is alone and unprotected. Pursue her no further. Go back to London, marry your Lady Sefton, inherit your fortune, but leave Charmian Brown in peace."

"And pray," he said, frowning suddenly, "why this solicitude on her behalf? What is she to you, this Charmian Brown?"

"Nothing, nothing at all, God knows, nor ever can she be. . . ."

Sir Maurice leaned suddenly forward, and, catching me by the shoulder, peered into my face.

"By Heavens!" he exclaimed. "The fellow actually loves her!"

"Well? Why not? Yes, I love her."

A furious rage seemed suddenly to possess him; the languid, smiling gentleman became a devil with vicious eyes and evil, snarling mouth, whose fingers sank into my flesh as he swung me backwards and forwards in a powerful grip.

"You love her? You? You?"

"Yes," I answered, flinging him off so that he staggered. "Yes—yes! I, who fought for her once, and am willing—most willing—to do so again, now or at any other time, for though I hold no hope of winning her ever, yet I can serve her still, and protect her from the pollution of your presence."

I clenched my fists.

He stood posed as though about to spring at me, and I saw his knuckles gleam whiter than the laces above them, but all at once he laughed lightly, easily as ever.

"How like you, worthy cousin, how very like you, and how affecting! But I tell you, she is mine—mine—and always has been, and no man living shall come between us—no, by God!"

"That remains to be seen!"

"Ha?"

"Though, indeed, I think she is safe from you while I live."

"But then, Cousin Peter, life is a very uncertain thing at best."

Sir Maurice strolled to the door, and being there, paused, and looked back over his shoulder.

"I go to find Charmian," he said. "And I shall find her—sooner or later—and when I do, should you take it upon yourself to—to come between us again, or presume to interfere again, I shall kill you, worthy cousin, without the least compunction. If you think this sufficient warning, act upon it; if not . . ."

He shrugged his shoulders significantly.

"Farewell, good and worthy Cousin Peter, farewell—or shall we say *au revoir?*"

* * *

Returning to my cottage, I could hardly bear the emptiness of it with Charmian gone.

My depression grew throughout the next few days, and my spirits reached their lowest ebb, until one evening as I sat alone in the cottage, strange and morbid fancies began to come into my head.

My eyes wandered to an iron hook projecting from the wall above the door, and, as if led by some strange compunction, I began to loosen the handkerchief that was knotted about my neck.

"Peter!" a voice cried. "Peter!" And a hand was beating upon the door.

She came in swiftly, closing the door behind her, found and lit a candle, and, setting it upon the table between us, put back the hood of her cloak and looked at me, while I stood mute before her, embarrassed by the accusation in her eyes.

"Coward!" she said.

With the word she snatched the neckerchief from my grasp, and, casting it upon the floor, set her foot upon it.

"Yes, I was lost in a great darkness, and full of a horror of coming nights and days, and so I would have run away from it all, like a coward. . . ."

"Oh, hateful . . . hateful!" she cried, and covered her face as from some horror.

"Indeed, you cannot despise me more than I do myself," I said, "now or ever. I am a failure in all things, except perhaps the making of horseshoes, and this world has no place for failures, and as for horseshoes . . ."

"Fool," she whispered. "Oh, coward that seemed so brave and strong. Oh, man that was so gloriously young and unspoiled, that it should end here . . . that it should ever come to this!"

Although she kept her face hidden, I knew that she was weeping.

"A woman's love transforms the man till she sees him, not as he is but as her heart would have him be; the dross becomes pure gold, and she believes, and believes, until . . . one day her heart breaks. . . ."

"Charmian! What—what do you mean?"

"Oh, are you still so blind? Must I tell you? Why did I live beside you here in the wilderness? Why did I work for you . . . contrive for you . . . and seek to make this desolation a home for you?

"Often my heart cried out its secret to you, but you never heard; often it trembled in my voice, looked at you from my eyes . . . but you never guessed. And you drove me from you with shameful words . . . but . . . oh! . . . I came back to you. And now . . . even yet . . ."

She stopped, suddenly, and once more hid her face from me in her hands.

"And—even yet, Charmian?"

"I am so weak . . . so weak! I hate myself."

"Charmian!" I cried. "Oh Charmian!"

I seized her hands and, despite her resistance, drew her into my arms; and, clasping her close, I forced her to look at me.

"And even yet? What more—what more—tell me!"

"Don't!" she cried. "Don't! You shame me . . . let me go."

"God knows I am all unworthy, Charmian, and so low in my abasement that to touch you is presumption, but oh, woman whom I have loved from the first, and shall to the end. Have you stooped in your infinite mercy, to lift me from these depths—is it a new life you offer me—was it for this you came tonight?"

"Let me go. . . . Oh, Peter! Let me go."

"Why, why did you come?"

"Loose me!"

"Why did you come?"

"To meet Sir Maurice Vibart."

"To meet Sir Maurice?"

And in that moment she broke from me, and stood with her head thrown back, and her eyes were very bright, as though defying me. But I remained where I was, my arms hanging.

"He was to meet me here . . . at nine o'clock."

178

"Oh, Charmian, are all women so cruel as you, I wonder?"

Turning my back upon her, I leaned above the mantel, staring down at the long-dead ashes in the hearth.

But, standing there, I heard a footstep outside, and swung round with clenched fists, yet Charmian was quicker, and, as the door opened and Sir Maurice entered, she was between us.

He stood upon the threshold, dazzled a little by the light, but smiling, graceful, as debonaire as ever. Indeed, his very presence seemed to make the mean room meaner by contrast.

As he bent to kiss her hand, I became acutely conscious of my own rough person, my worn and shabby clothes, and of my hands, coarsened and grimed by labour; wherefore my frown grew the blacker and I clenched my fists the tighter.

"I lost my way, Charmian, but, though late, I am nonetheless welcome, I trust? Ah, you frown, Cousin Peter?"

"You have already met, then?" enquired Charmian, glancing from one to the other of us.

"We had that mutual pleasure nearly a week ago, when we agreed to—disagree, as we always have done, and shall do—with the result that we find each other agreeably disagreeable."

"I had hoped that you might be friends."

"My dear Charmian—I wonder at you. But I am not here on Cousin Peter's account. I have come for you, Charmian, because I love you. I have sought you patiently until I found you, and I will never let you go as long as life lasts.

"I have been very patient, Charmian, submitting to your whims and fancies, but through it all I knew—and in your woman's heart, you knew—that you must yield at last, that the chase must end—someday; well, let it be tonight; my chaise is waiting. . . ."

"When I ran away from you in the storm, Sir Maurice, I told you, once and for all, that I hated you. Have you forgotten? Hated you! Always and forever! And I tried to . . . kill you. . . ."

"Oh, Charmian! I have known such hate transfigured into love, before now—such love as is only worth the winning. And you are mine, you always were, from the moment that our eyes met. Come, my chaise is waiting; in a few hours we can be in London or Dover. . . ."

"No . . . never!"

"Never is a long time, Charmian—but I am at your service. What is your will?"

"I shall remain . . . here."

"Here? In the wilderness?"

"With my . . . husband."

"Your husband?"

"I am going to marry your cousin . . . Peter Vibart."

The pipe slipped from my fingers and shattered to pieces on the floor, and in that same fraction of time Sir Maurice had turned and leapt towards me.

But as he came I struck him twice, with left and right, and he staggered backwards to the wall. He stood for a moment, with his head stooped upon his hands.

When he looked up his face was dead white, and with a smear of blood upon it that seemed to accentuate its pallor; but his voice came smooth and unruffled as ever.

"The Feminine Mind is given to change," he said softly. "I shall return—yes, I shall come back. Smile, Madam! Triumph, cousin! But I shall come between you yet, I tell you, I'll come between you —living or—dead!"

And so he turned, and was gone into the shadows.

But, as for me, I sat down and stared down at the broken fragments of my pipe.

"Peter?"

"You are safe now, he is gone—but oh, Charmian, was there no other way?"

She was down beside me on her knees, had taken my hand, rough and grimy as it was, and pressed it to her lips, and so had drawn it about her neck, holding it there, and with her face hidden in my breast.

"Oh ... strong man who is so weak!" she whispered. "Oh, grave philosopher who is so foolish! Oh, lonely boy who is so helpless. Oh, Peter Vibart ... my Peter!"

"Charmian? What does it mean?"

"It means, Peter . . ."

"Yes?"

"That . . . the . . . Humble Person . . ."

"Yes?"

"Will . . . marry you, whenever you will . . . if . . ."

"Yes?"

"If you will . . . only . . . ask her."

Chapter
Eight

Now, as the little Preacher closed his book, the sun rose up, filling the world about us with its glory.

And looking into the eyes of my wife, it seemed that a veil was lifted, for a moment there, and I read that which her lips might never tell; and there also was joy and shame, and a deep happiness.

"See," said the little Preacher, smiling upon us, "it is day and a very glorious one. Go forth together, Man and Wife, upon this great wide road that we call Life; go forth together, made strong in Faith, and brave with Hope, and the memory of Him, who walked these ways before you."

And so we turned together, side by side, and left him standing amidst his roses.

And on reaching, at length, the Hollow, Charmian paused beside the pool among the willows to view herself in the pellucid water. And in this mirror our eyes met. Suddenly her lashes dropped and she turned her head aside.

"Don't, Peter!" she whispered. "Don't look at me so."

"How can I help it when you are so beautiful?"

Because of my eyes, she would have fled from me, but I caught her in my arms, and there among the leaves, despite the jealous babble of the brook, for the second time in my life her lips met mine.

And, still gazing into her eyes, I told her how, in this shady bower, I had once watched her weaving leaves into her hair, and heard her talk to her reflection, and so had stolen away for fear of her beauty.

"Fear, Peter?"

"We were so far out of the world, and I longed to kiss you."

"And didn't, Peter."

"And didn't, Charmian, because we were so very far from the world, and because you were so very much alone, and . . ."

"And because, Peter, because you are a gentleman and strong, as the old locket says. And do you remember," she went on hurriedly, laying her cool, restraining fingers on my eager lips, "how I found you wearing that locket, and how you

184

blundered and stammered over it, and pretended to read your Homer?"

"And how you sang to prevent me?"

"And how gravely you reproved me?"

"And how you called me a 'creature'?"

"And how you deserved it, and grew more helpless and ill at ease than ever, and how, just to flatter my vanity, you told me I had 'glorious hair'?"

"And so you have," I said, kissing a curl at her temple. "When you unbind it, my Charmian, it will cover you—like a mantle."

Now when I said this, for some reason she glanced up at me, sudden and shy, and blushed and slipped from my arms, and fled up the path like a nymph.

We presently entered the cottage, flushed and laughing with sheer happiness. She rolled up her sleeves and set about preparing breakfast, laughing my assistance to scorn, but growing mightily indignant when I kissed her, yet blushing, and yielding nevertheless.

"Oh, Charmian! How wonderful you are!" I sighed. "Surely no woman ever had such beautiful arms! So round, and soft, and white, Charmian."

She turned upon me with a fork held up admonishingly; but, meeting my look, her eyes wavered, and up from throat to brow rushed a wave of burning crimson.

"Oh, Peter! You make me . . . almost . . . afraid

of you," she whispered, and hid her face against my shoulder.

"Are you content to have married such a very poor man, to be the wife of a village black-smith?"

"Why, Peter . . . in all the world there never was such another blacksmith as mine, and . . . and . . . there! The kettle is boiling over. . . ."

"Let it!" I said.

"And the bacon . . . the bacon will burn . . . let me go, and . . . oh, Peter!"

So, in due time, we sat down to our solitary wedding breakfast; and there were no eyes to speculate upon the bride's beauty, to note her changing colour, or the glory of her eyes.

No health was proposed, nor toasts drunk, nor any speeches spoken—except, perhaps, by my good friend, the brook outside.

In this solitude we were surely closer togeth-er, and belonged more fully to each other, for all her looks and thoughts were mine, as mine were hers.

So the golden hours slipped by, the sun crept westwards, and evening stole upon us.

"This is a very rough place for you," I said, and sighed.

We were sitting on the bench before the door, and Charmian had laid her folded hands upon my shoulder, and her chin was upon her hands. And now she echoed my sigh, but an-swered without stirring:

"It is the dearest place in all the world."

"And very lonely!" I pursued.

"I shall be busy all day long, Peter, and you always reach home as evening falls, and then ... then ... oh! I shan't be lonely."

"But I am such a gloomy fellow at the best of times, and very clumsy, Charmian, and something of a failure."

"And ... my husband."

"Peter, oh, Peter!" a voice called.

Charmian stole her arms about my neck.

"I think it is Simon," I said uneasily. "What can have brought him? I must go and see what he wants."

"Yes, Peter," she murmured, but the clasp of her arms tightened.

"What is it?" I said, looking into her troubled eyes. "Charmian, you are trembling! What is it?"

"I don't know ... but oh, Peter! I feel as if a shadow, a black and awful shadow, were creeping upon us, hiding us from each other. I am very foolish, aren't I? And this, our wedding day!"

"Peter! Peter!"

"Come with me, Charmian; let us go together."

"No, I must wait, it is woman's destiny to wait, but I am brave now; go ... see what is wanted."

I found Simon, sure enough, in the lane,

seated in his cart, and his face looked squarer and grimmer even than usual.

"Oh, Peter!" he said, gripping my hand. "It's come at last—Gaffer be going."

"Going, Simon?"

"Dying, Peter. Fell downstairs this morning. Doctor says he can't last the day out—sinking fast he is, and he is asking for you, Peter. You weren't at work this morning, Peter, so I came to fetch you—you'll come back with me to bid good-bye to the old man?"

"Yes, I'll come, Simon," I answered; "wait here for me."

Charmian was waiting for me in the cottage, and as she looked up at me I saw that the trouble was back in her eyes again.

"You must ... go ... leave me?" she enquired.

"For a little while."

"Yes ... I ... I felt it," she said with a pitiful little smile.

"The Ancient is dying," I said.

"Oh, Peter ... don't go ... don't leave me!" cried Charmian suddenly, and I saw that her face was very pale, and that she trembled.

"Charmian!" I said, and sprang to her side. "Oh, my love, what is it?"

"It is as though the shadow hung over us, darker and more threatening, Peter; as if our happiness were at an end. I seem to hear Maurice's threat to come between us ... living or ...

188

dead. I am afraid!" she whispered, clinging to me. "I am afraid!"

But all at once she was calm again, and full of self-reproaches, calling herself "weak" and "foolish" and "hysterical," "though, indeed, I was never hysterical before!" and telling me that I must go to the "gentle, dying old man."

She urged me to the door, almost eagerly, till, being out of the cottage, she started trembling once more, and wound her arms round my neck with a great sob.

"Oh, will you come back soon . . . very soon, Peter? And we know that nothing can ever come between us again, never again, my husband."

And with that blessed word she drew me down to her lips, and turning, fled into the cottage.

I went on slowly up the path to meet Simon, and as I went my heart was heavy and my mind full of a strange foreboding.

* * *

As I walked home, some hours later, my thoughts turned gradually from the old man, now lying at peace, to the woman waiting for me.

My heart rose as I drew nearer to the cottage. Then a sound broke upon the stillness, sudden and sharp, like the snapping of a stick.

I stopped and glanced about me, but it had come and gone, lost in the all-pervading calm.

So I began to descend the leafy path. But all

at once I stopped, staring at something which lay at the edge of a pool of moonlight—a white claw —a hand whose fingers, talon-like, had sunk deep and embedded themselves in the turf.

And beyond this gleaming hand was an arm, and beyond that again something that baulked across my path, darker than the shadows.

Running forward, I stood looking down at that which lay at my feet, and started back in shuddering horror.

For in those features, hideous with blood, stained and blackened with powder, I recognised my cousin—Sir Maurice.

Then, remembering the stick that had snapped, I wondered no more, but a sudden deadly faintness came upon me so that I leaned weakly against a tree nearby.

A rustling of leaves—a shuddering breath— and though I did not raise my head, I knew that Charmian was there.

"Oh, Peter!" she whispered. "Oh, Peter!" And that was all; but, moved by something in her tone, I glanced up.

Her eyes were wide and staring, not at me but at that which lay between us. Her face was pallid, even her lips had lost their colour, and she clasped one hand upon her bosom—the other was hidden in the folds of her gown.

I reached out and caught that hidden hand, and drew the weapon from her nerveless fingers, holding it where the light could play upon it.

She started, shivered violently, and covered her eyes, while I, looking down at this pistol in my hand, saw that it had recently been fired.

"He has kept his word! He has kept his word!"

"Yes, Charmian, he has kept his word!"

"Oh, Peter!" she said, and moaned, and stretched out her hands towards me.

Yet she kept her face turned from that which lay across the path between us, and her hands were shaking pitifully.

"No, Peter, no . . . oh, God . . . you do not think it . . . you can't . . . you mustn't. I was alone, waiting for you . . . and the hours passed and you didn't come . . . and I was frightened. I thought I heard someone creeping round the cottage.

"Once I thought someone peered in at the lattice, and once I thought someone tried the door. And so . . . because I was frightened, Peter, I took that . . . that, and held it in my hand, Peter. And while I sat there, it seemed more than ever . . . that somebody was breathing softly . . . outside the door.

"And so, Peter, I couldn't bear it any more and opened the lattice, and fired . . . in the air . . . I swear it was in the air. And I stood there at the open casement . . . sick with fear, and trying to pray for you because I knew he had come back . . . to kill you Peter.

"And while I prayed, I heard another shot . . . not close, but faint . . . like the snapping of a twig, Peter . . . and I ran out . . . and . . . oh, Peter . . .

that is all...but you believe...oh...you believe, don't you, Peter?"

While she spoke, I had slipped the pistol into my pocket, and now I held out my hands to her and drew her near, and gazed into the troubled depths of her eyes.

"Charmian!" I said. "Charmian...I love you! And God forbid that I should ever doubt you any more."

With a sigh she sank into my embrace, her arms crept about my neck, and our lips met, and clung together.

But even then, while I looked upon her beauty, while the contact of her lips thrilled through me, even then in my mind I saw the murderous pistol in her hand, as I had seen it months ago.

Indeed, it almost seemed that she divined my thought, for she drew swiftly back and looked up at me with haggard eyes.

"Peter," she whispered, "what is it...what is it?"

"Oh, Charmian," I said, over and over again, "I love you, I love you."

I kissed her appealing eyes, and stayed her questioning lips with my kisses.

"I love you more than my life, more than honour, more than my soul; and, because I love you so, tonight you must leave me...."

"Leave you? Ah...no, Peter, I am your wife ...I must stay with you...to suffer and share your troubles and dangers. Let us go away together ... now ... anywhere, anywhere, only let us be together ... my ... husband."

"Don't! Don't! Do you think it is so easy to remain here without you, to lose you so soon? You see, before the week is out my description will be all over England; we should be caught, and you would have to stand beside me in a Court of Justice, and face the shame of it. . . ."

"Dear love! It would be my pride, Peter, to face them all ... to clasp this dear hand in mine. . . ."

"Never!" I cried, clenching my fists. "Never! You must leave me; no one must know Charmian Brown ever existed ... you must go!"

"Hush!" she whispered, clasping me tighter. "Listen ... someone is coming. Come, let us go and meet him."

"No, Charmian, no, I must see this man alone. You must leave here, tonight—now. You can catch the London Mail at the crossroads. Go to Blackheath, to Sir Richard Anstruther, he is my friend, tell him everything. . . ."

She was down at my feet, and had caught my hand to her bosom.

"I can't! I can't go and leave you here alone. I have loved you so ... from the very first, and it seems that each day my love has grown until it is part of me. Oh, Peter! Don't send me away from you ... it will kill me, I think. . . ."

"Better that than the shame of a prison!" I

exclaimed; and while I spoke I lifted her in my arms. "Oh, I am proud, proud to have won such a love as yours. Let me try to be worthy of it. Good-bye, my beloved!"

I kissed her, and would have turned away but her arms clung about me.

"Oh, Peter! If you must go . . . if you will go, call me . . . your wife . . . just once, Peter."

I stooped above her cold hands and kissed her trembling fingers.

"Someday, if there is a just God in Heaven, we shall meet again; perhaps soon, perhaps not. Until then, let us dream of that glorious, golden someday; but now—farewell, oh, beloved wife!"

With a broken cry, she drew my hand down upon her breast, and clasped it there, while her tears mingled with her kisses, and so, crying my name, she turned, and was lost among the leaves.

*　　*　　*

"Hallo!"

"Hallo!" I called back. "This way, this way!"

I saw the figure of a man whom I at once recognised as the one-time postillion, bearing the lanthorn of a chaise, and as he approached, it struck me that this meeting was very much like our first, save for him who lay in the shadows, staring up at me with unwinking eyes.

"So, ho!" exclaimed the postillion as he came up, raising his lanthorn that he could see me better. "It's you again, is it?"

"Yes!"

He stepped nearer, lowering his lanthorn, then staggered blindly backwards.

"Lord love me!" And he stood, staring, with dropped jaw.

"Where is your chaise?"

"Up yonder, yonder in the lane."

"Then help me to carry him there."

"No, no, I dare not touch it—I can't—not me —not me!"

"I think you will," I said, and took the pistol from my pocket.

"He isn't likely to come to this time, I'm thinking!" said the postillion, mopping the sweat from his brow, and grinning with pallid lips, after we had got our burden into the vehicle.

"What now?" he asked.

"Now you can drive us to Cranbrook."

"What—are you coming too?"

"Yes," I nodded, "yes, I am coming too."

"Lord love me!" he exclaimed, and a moment later I heard him chirruping to his horses. The whip cracked and the chaise lurched forward.

And so at last we pulled up before the Posting House at Cranbrook. Looking from the window, I saw a ring of faces with eyes that gleamed in the light of the lanthorns, and every eye was fixed on me.

I saw the postillion push his way to the steps of the Inn, and turn there, with hands clenched and raised above his head.

"My master, Sir Maurice Vibart, is killed—shot to death—murdered down there in the haunted Hollow! And if you asks me who done it, I says to you—he did—so help me God!"

So speaking, he raised his whip and pointed at me.

And every moment the murmur swelled, and grew more threatening; fists were clenched and sticks flourished. But suddenly the crowd was burst asunder and Black George stood beside me, his eyes glowing, his fists clenched, and his hair and beard bristling.

"Stand back, you chaps," he growled, "stand back, or I'll hurt some of you. What's the matter with the fools, Peter?"

"Matter?" cried the postillion. "Murder is the matter! My master is murdered—shot to death—and there stands the man that did it!"

Now, as he spoke, the crowd parted, and four ostlers appeared, bearing a hurdle between them, and on the hurdle lay a figure, an elegant figure whose head and face were still muffled in my neckerchief.

I saw George start, and like a flash his glance came round to my bare throat, and dismay was in his eyes.

"Oh, Peter!" he whispered. "Speak! Speak!"

"Not here, George. It would be of no avail; besides, I can say nothing to clear myself."

"Nothing, Peter?"

"Nothing, George. This man was shot and killed in the Hollow, I found him lying dead. I found the empty pistol, and the postillion, over there, found me standing over the body. That is all I have to tell."

"Peter, oh, Peter! Let's run for it—it would be easy for the likes of you and me. . . ."

"No, George, it would be worse than useless. But one thing I do ask of you—you know me so much better than most—and it is that you will bid me good-bye, and take my hand once more, George, here, before all these eyes that look upon me as a murderer, and . . ."

Before I could finish speaking, rough hands were laid upon mine. I saw George's fist raised threateningly, but caught it in my grasp.

"Good-bye," I said. "Good-bye, George, and don't look so downcast, man."

But we were forced apart, and I was pushed and pulled and hustled away.

And thus in much estate I ascended a flight of worn stone steps into the churchyard, and so came at last to the great square church-tower, into which I was incontinently thrust, and there very securely locked up until the following morning, when I was bundled into a chaise and driven off.

* * *

We had been driving for some time, and my two guards were talking amongst themselves and sharing a bottle of rum, when suddenly the chaise lurched violently.

There was a cry, a splintering of glass, a crash, and I was lying half-stunned in a ditch, listening to the chorus of oaths and cries that rose from the cloud of dust where the frightened horses reared and plunged.

How long I remained thus I cannot say, but all at once I found myself upon my feet, running down the road, for, hazy though my mind yet was, I could think only of escape, of liberty and freedom at any price—at any cost.

So I ran on down the road, somewhat unsteadily as yet, because my fall had been a heavy one, and my brain still reeled.

I heard a shot behind me, the sharp crack of a pistol, and a bullet sang over my head; and then I knew they were after me, for I could hear the patter of their feet upon the hard road.

Somehow I managed to outstrip them and gradually the footsteps behind me died away and I found myself alone in strange countryside.

I walked and walked, and presently as I went I heard the merry ring and clink of hammer and anvil, and, guided by the sound, I came to a tumble-down smithy where was a man busily at work, with a red-headed boy at the bellows.

Seeing me, the smith set down his hammer and stared open-mouthed, as did the red-headed boy.

"How long would it take you to file off these shackles?" I enquired, holding out my hands.

"To—to file them off?"

"Yes."

"Why, that—that—depends . . . "

"Then do it as soon as you can."

But he progressed so slowly, for one reason and another, that I began to grow impatient; moreover, noticing that the red-headed boy had disappeared, I bade him desist.

"A cold chisel and hammer will be quickest. Come, cut me off this chain—here, close up to the rivets."

When he had done this, I took his file and, thrusting it beneath my coat, set off, running my hardest, leaving him to stare after me, with his eyes and mouth wider than ever.

The sun was down when I reached the woods, and here in the kind shadows I stayed to rest awhile, and rid myself of my handcuffs; but when I felt for the file to do so—it was gone.

* * *

It was upon the third night since my escape that, faint and spent with hunger, I overtook something that crawled in the gloom of the hedge, and approaching, pistol in hand, saw that it was a man.

He was creeping forward slowly and painfully on his hands and knees, but all at once he sank down, with his face in the grass, only to rise, groaning, and creep on once more. And as he went I heard him praying:

"Lord, give me strength. O Lord, give me strength. It is so far—so far. . . ." And, groaning, he sank down again upon his face.

"You are ill!" I said, bending over him.

"I must reach Deptford, she's buried at Deptford, and I shall die tonight. . . . O Lord, give me strength!" He panted.

"Deptford is miles away," I said.

Now as I spoke he lifted himself upon his hands and stared up at me.

"You!" he cried, and spat up in the air towards me. "Devil Vibart!"

I recoiled instinctively before the man's sudden, wild ferocity, but propping himself against the bank he shook his hand at me, and laughed.

"Devil! Shade! Ghost of a devil—have you come back to see me die?"

"Who are you?" I cried, bending to look into the pale, emaciated face. "Who are you?"

"A shadow, a ghost, a phantom, as you are. But my name was Strickland once, as yours was Devil Vibart. I am changed of late, you said so in the Hollow, and laughed. You don't laugh now, Devil Vibart, you remember poor John Strickland now.

"Yes, I was a shadow that was always behind you, following and following you, Satan Vibart, tracking and tracking you to hell and damnation. And you fled here, and you fled there, but I was always behind you. You hid from me among lowly folk, but you could not escape the shadow.

"Many times I would have killed you, but she was between—the Woman. I came once to your cottage, it was night, and the door opened beneath my hand, but your time was not then.

"I met you among trees, as I did once before, and I told you my name as I did once before, and I spoke of her you ruined, of Angela, and cried her name—and shot you, just here, above the brow; and so you died, Devil Vibart, as soon I must, for my mission is accomplished. . . ."

"It was you!" I cried, kneeling beside him. "It was your hand that shot Sir Maurice Vibart?"

"Yes," he answered, his voice growing very gentle as he went on, "for Angela's sake—my dead wife."

Fumbling in his pocket, he drew out a woman's small, lace-edged handkerchief, and I saw that it was thickened and black with blood.

"This was hers," he continued, "in her hand, the night she died—I had meant to lay it on her grave—the blood of atonement—but now . . ."

Suddenly there was a crash in the hedge above, and I was down upon my knees, with fingers clasped round my throat.

"I've got him—this way—quick!"

My fist drove into his ribs; I struggled up

under a rain of blows and we struck and swayed, and staggered and struck, trampling the groaning wretch who lay dying in the ditch.

Before me was the pale oval of a face, and I hit it twice with my pistol-butt, and it was gone, and I was running along the road.

"Charmian spoke the truth! O God, I thank you!"

I burst through a hedge, running on and on, careless alike of being seen, of capture or escape, of prison or freedom, for in my heart was a great joy.

I was conscious of shouts and cries, but I heeded them no more, listening only to the song of happiness my heart was singing.

"Charmian spoke the truth, her hands are clean. O God, I thank you!"

And so I once more turned my face London-wards.

But then the mist seemed to get into my brain and all things were hazy.

A great house lay before me, with lighted windows here and there.

Then I took out my clasp-knife, and, fumbling blindly, put back the catch (as I had often done as a boy), and so, the window opening, I clambered into the dimness beyond.

I stumbled forward and my hand touched something, a long dark object that was covered with a cloth, and, hardly knowing what I did, I drew back this cloth and looked down at that which it had covered, and I sank down upon my knees, groaning.

For there, staring up at me, cold, contemptuous and set like marble, was the smiling, dead face of Cousin Maurice.

As I knelt there, I was conscious that the door had opened, that someone approached, bearing a light, but I did not move or heed.

"Peter? Good God in Heaven! Is it Peter?"

I looked up into the dilated eyes of Sir Richard.

"Is it really Peter?" he whispered.

"Yes, Sir—dying, I think."

"No, no, Peter, dear boy," he stammered. "You didn't know—you hadn't heard—poor Maurice —murdered—fellow—name of Smith!"

"Yes, Sir Richard, I know more about it than most. You see, I am Peter Smith."

Sir Richard fell back from me, and I saw the candles swaying in his grasp.

"You?" he whispered. "You? Oh, Peter! Oh, my boy!"

"But I am innocent, innocent—you believe me—you, who were my earliest friend, my good, kind friend—you believe me?"

I stretched out my hands appealingly, but as I did so the light fell gleaming upon my shameful wristlets, and even as we gazed into each other's eyes, mute and breathless, came the sound of steps and hushed voices.

Sir Richard sprang forward, and, catching

me in a powerful grip, half-led, half-dragged me behind a tall leather screen beside the hearth, and thrusting me into a chair, turned and hurried to meet the intruders.

Here the mist settled down upon my brain once more, and I heard nothing but a confused murmur of voices, and it seemed to me that I was back on the road again, hemmed in by those gibbering phantoms that spoke so much, and yet said but one word: "Murder."

"Quick—a candle here—a candle—bring a light...."

There came a glare before my smarting eyes, and I struggled up to my feet.

"Gentlemen, I'll lay my life the murderer is found—though how he should come here of all places—extraordinary. Sir Richard, you and I, as Magistrates—duty..."

But the mist was very thick, and the voices grew confused again; only I knew that hands were upon me, that I was led into another room, where there were lights that glittered upon the silver, the decanters, and the glasses of a supper-table.

"Yes," I was saying, slowly and heavily; "yes, I am Peter Smith, a blacksmith, who escaped from his gaolers on the Tonbridge Road, but I am innocent, before God, I am innocent. And now, do with me as you will, for I am very weary...."

Sir Richard's arm was about me, and his

voice sounded in my ears, but as though from a great way off:

"Sirs," he said, "this is my friend—Sir Peter Vibart."

There was a moment's pause, then a chair fell with a crash, and there rose a confusion of excited voices, yet which grew suddenly silent, for the door had opened.

On the threshold stood a woman, tall and proud, and richly dressed, from the little dusty boots that peeped beneath her habit to the wide-sweeping hat-brim that shaded the high beauty of her face. And I would have gone to her, only my strength failed me.

"Charmian!"

She started, and turning, uttered a cry and ran to me.

"Charmian," I said, "oh, Charmian."

So with her tender arms about me and her kisses on my lips, the mist settled down upon me, thicker and darker than ever.

* * *

A bright room, luxuriously appointed; a great wide bed with carved posts and embroidered canopy; between the curtained windows, a tall oak press with grotesque heads carved on it, heads that leered and gaped and scowled at me.

But the bed and the room and the oak press were all familiar, and the grotesque heads had leered and gaped and frowned on me before, and haunted my boyish dreams many and many a night.

And now I lay between sleeping and waking, staring dreamily at all these things, till, roused by a voice nearby, and starting up, broad awake, I saw Sir Richard.

"Deuce take you, Peter! A nice pickle you've made of yourself, with your infernal Revolutionary notions, your digging and blacksmithing, your walking-tours . . ."

"Where is she, Sir Richard?" I broke in. "Pray, where is she?"

"She?"

"She who I saw last night. . . ."

"You were asleep last night, and the night before."

"Asleep? Then how long have I been here?"

"Three days, Peter."

"And where is she? Surely I have not dreamed it all! Where is Charmian?"

"She went away, this morning."

"Gone! Where to?"

"Gad, Peter! How should I know?"

But, seeing the distress in my face, he smiled, and tendered me the letter.

"She left this 'For Peter, when he awoke,' and I've been waiting for Peter to wake all the morning."

Hastily I broke the seal, and unfolding the paper with tremulous hands, read:

Dearest, noblest and most disbelieving of Peters,

Oh, did you think you could hide your hateful suspicion from me ... from me, who knows you so well? I felt it in your kiss, in the touch of your strong hand, I saw it in your eyes.

Even when I told you the truth, and begged you to believe me, even then, deep down in your heart, you thought it was my hand that had killed Sir Maurice, and God only knows the despair that filled me as I turned and left you.

And so, Peter ... perhaps to punish you a little, perhaps because I cannot bear the noisy world just yet, perhaps because I fear you a little ... I have run away. But I remember also how, believing me guilty, you loved me still, and gave yourself up, to shield me, and, dying of hunger and fatigue ... came to find me.

And so, Peter, I have not run so very far, nor hidden myself so very close, and if you understand me as you should, your search need not be so very long.

And dear, dear, Peter, there is just one other thing, which I hoped that you would guess, which any other would have guessed, but which, being a philosopher, you never did guess.

Oh, Peter ... I was once, very long ago it

*seems, Sophia Charmian Sefton, but I am now,
and always was, Your Humble Person,*

Charmian

The letter fell from my fingers, and I remained staring before me so long that Sir Richard came and laid his hand on my shoulder.

"Oh, boy! She has told me all the story, and
I think, Peter, I think it is given to very few men
to win the love of such a woman as this."

"God knows it!"

"And to have married one so very noble and
high in all things, you should be very proud, Peter."

"I am. Oh, I am, Sir."

"Even, Peter, even though she be a virago,
this Lady Sophia, or a termagant ..."

"I was a great fool in those days," I said,
hanging my head, "and very young!"

"It was only six months ago, Peter."

"But I am years older today, Sir."

*　　*　　*

It was with a certain satisfaction that I once
more donned buckskin and spurred boots, and
noticed moreover how tight my coat was across
the shoulders; yet I dressed hastily, for my mind
was already on the road, galloping to Charmian.

In the library I found Sir Richard and Mr.

Grainger, who greeted me with his precise little bow.

"I have to congratulate you, Sir Peter," he began, "not only on your distinguished marriage and accession to fortune, but upon the fact that the—ah—unpleasantness connecting a certain Peter Smith with your unfortunate cousin's late decease has been entirely removed by means of the murderer's written confession, placed in my hands some days ago by the Lady Sophia. . . ."

"A written confession, and she brought it to you?"

"Galloped all the way from Tonbridge, by God!"

"It seems that the man, John Strickland by name, lodged with a certain Preacher to whom, in Lady Vibart's presence, he confessed his crime, and willingly wrote out a deposition to that effect.

"It also appears that the man, sick though he was, wandered from the Preacher's cottage, and was eventually found upon the road, and now lies in Maidstone gaol, in a dying condition."

Chancing presently to look from the window, I saw a groom who led a horse up and down before the door.

"You are going to find her, Peter?" Sir Richard asked.

"Yes, Sir."

"And you know where to look?"

"I shall go to a certain cottage."

"Then you'd better go, boy."

He followed me out to the drive, where I mounted the mare.

"I always felt very fatherly towards you, Peter, and you won't forget the lonely old man—come and see me now and then, both of you, for it does get damnably lonely here sometimes, and, oh, curse it! Good-bye, dear lad!"

So he turned and walked up the steps into his great, lonely house.

*   *   *

All day I rode, retracing my way to Sissinghurst.

On reaching the Hollow, I paused to glance about me as I always did before descending that leafy path; and the shadows were very black and a chill wind stirred among the leaves.

I shivered, and wondered, for the first time, if I had done right—if the cottage had been in Charmian's mind when she wrote.

Then I descended the path, hurrying past a certain dark spot. And coming at last within sight of the cottage, I paused again and shivered again, for the windows were dark and the door shut.

But the latch yielded readily beneath my hand, so I went in, and closed and locked the door behind me.

For, upon the hearth a fire burned with a

dim, red glow that filled the place with shadows, and the shadows were very deep.

"Charmian! Oh, Charmian, are you there—have I guessed right?"

I heard a rustle close beside me, and in the gloom came a hand to meet and clasp my own.

I stooped and kissed those slender fingers, drawing her into the fire glow, and her eyes were hidden by their lashes, and the glow of the fire seemed reflected in her cheeks.

"The candles were so . . . bright, Peter," she whispered.

"Yes."

"And so . . . when I heard you coming . . ."

"You heard me?"

"I was sitting on the bench, outside, Peter."

"And when you heard me, you put the candles out?"

"They seemed so . . . bright, Peter."

"And shut the door?"

"I only just closed it, Peter."

She was still wrapped in her cloak, as she had been when I first saw her, wherefore I put back the hood from her face. And behold! As I did so, her hair fell down, rippling over my arm, and covering us both in its splendour, as it had done once before.

"Indeed, you have glorious hair! It seems wonderful to think that you are my wife. I can scarcely believe it—even now!"

"Why, I had meant that you should marry me from the first, Peter."

"Had you?"

"Do you think I should ever have come back to this dear solitude otherwise?"

Now, when I would have kissed her, she turned her head aside.

"Peter."

"Yes, Charmian?"

"The Lady Sophia Sefton never did gallop her horse up the steps of Saint Paul's Cathedral."

"Didn't she, Charmian?"

"And she couldn't help her name being bandied from mouth to mouth, or 'hiccoughed out over slopping wine-glasses,' could she?"

"No," I said, frowning. "What a vasty young fool I was!"

"And, Peter . . ."

"Well, Charmian?"

"She never was . . . and never will be . . . buxom, or strapping . . . will she? 'Buxom' is such a . . . hateful word, Peter! And you . . . love her? Wait, Peter . . . as much as ever you loved Charmian Brown?"

"Yes," I said, "yes."

"And . . . nearly as much as . . . your dream woman?"

"More, much more, because you are the embodiment of all my dreams, you always will be, Charmian. Because I honour you for your intellect; and worship you for your gentleness, and

212

spotless purity. Because I love you with all my strength for your warm, sweet womanhood, and because you are beautiful, proud. . . ."

"And because, Peter, I am . . . just . . . your loving . . . Humble Person."

      ❋   ❋   ❋

Thus it was I went forth a fool, and toiled, and suffered, and loved, and in the end got me some little wisdom.

And thus did I, all unworthy as I am, win the heart of a noble woman whose love I pray will endure, even as mine will, when we shall have journeyed to the end of this Broad Highway, which is Life, and into the mystery of the Beyond.

ABOUT THE EDITOR

BARBARA CARTLAND, the world's most famous romantic novelist, who is also an historian, playwright, lecturer, political speaker and television personality, has now written over 200 books. She has also had many historical works published and has written four autobiographies as well as the biographies of her mother and that of her brother Ronald Cartland, who was the first Member of Parliament to be killed in the last war. This book has a preface by Sir Winston Churchill. Barbara Cartland has sold 80 million books over the world, more than half of these in the U.S.A. She broke the world record in 1975 by writing twenty books in a year, and her own record in 1976 with twenty-one. In private life, Barbara Cartland, who is a Dame of the Order of St. John of Jerusalem, has fought for better conditions and salaries for Midwives and Nurses. As President of the Royal College of Midwives (Hertfordshire Branch), she has been invested with the first Badge of Office ever given in Great Britain, which was subscribed to by the Midwives themselves. She has also championed the cause for old people and founded the first Romany Gypsy Camp in the world. Barbara Cartland is deeply interested in Vitamin Therapy and is President of the British National Association for Health.

Barbara Cartland's Library of Love

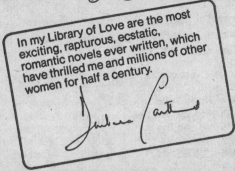

In my Library of Love are the most exciting, rapturous, ecstatic, romantic novels ever written, which have thrilled me and millions of other women for half a century.

Barbara Cartland

The World's Great Stories of Romance Specially Abridged by Barbara Cartland For Today's Readers.

☐	11487	THE SEQUENCE by Elinor Glyn	$1.50
☐	11468	THE BROAD HIGHWAY by Jeffrey Farnol	$1.50
☐	10927	THE WAY OF AN EAGLE by Ethel M. Dell	$1.50
☐	10926	THE REASON WHY by Elinor Glyn	$1.50
☐	10925	THE HUNDREDTH CHANCE by Ethel M. Dell	$1.50
☐	10527	THE KNAVE OF DIAMONDS by Ethel M. Dell	$1.50
☐	10506	A SAFETY MATCH by Ian Hay	$1.50
☐	10498	HIS HOUR by Elinor Glyn	$1.50
☐	11465	GREATHEART by Ethel M. Dell	$1.50
☐	11048	THE VICISSITUDES OF EVANGELINE by Elinor Glyn	$1.50
☐	11369	THE BARS OF IRON by Ethel M. Dell	$1.50
☐	11370	MAN AND MAID by Elinor Glyn	$1.50
☐	11391	THE SONS OF THE SHEIK by E. M. Hull	$1.50
☐	11376	SIX DAYS by Elinor Glyn	$1.50
☐	11466	RAINBOW IN THE SPRAY by Pamela Wayne	$1.50
☐	11467	THE GREAT MOMENT by Elinor Glyn	$1.50

Buy them at your local bookstore or use this handy coupon:

Barbara Cartland

The world's bestselling author of romantic fiction.
Her stories are always captivating tales of intrigue,
adventure and love.

☐	10972	LOOK, LISTEN AND LOVE	$1.50
☐	10975	A DUEL WITH DESTINY	$1.50
☐	10976	THE CURSE OF THE CLAN	$1.50
☐	2366	THE MASK OF LOVE	$1.25
☐	2426	AN ARROW OF LOVE	$1.25
☐	2433	A KISS FOR THE KING	$1.25
☐	2435	THE FRAGRANT FLOWER	$1.25
☐	2450	FIRE ON THE SNOW	$1.25
☐	2803	AN ANGEL IN HELL	$1.25
☐	2804	THE WILD CRY OF LOVE	$1.25
☐	2805	THE BLUE-EYED WITCH	$1.25
☐	2806	THE INCREDIBLE HONEYMOON	$1.25
☐	2950	THE SECRET OF THE GLEN	$1.25
☐	2987	CONQUERED BY LOVE	$1.25
☐	2993	NEVER LAUGH AT LOVE	$1.25
☐	10337	HUNGRY FOR LOVE	$1.25

Bantam Book Catalog

Here's your up-to-the-minute listing of every book currently available from Bantam.

This easy-to-use catalog is divided into categories and contains over 1400 titles by your favorite authors.

So don't delay—take advantage of this special opportunity to increase your reading pleasure.

Just send us your name and address and 25¢ (to help defray postage and handling costs).

BANTAM BOOKS, INC.
Dept. FC, 414 East Golf Road, Des Plaines, Ill. 60016

Mr./Mrs./Miss_____
(please print)

Address_____

City_____State_____Zip_____

Do you know someone who enjoys books? Just give us their names and addresses and we'll send them a catalog too!

Mr./Mrs./Miss_____

Address_____

City_____State_____Zip_____

Mr./Mrs./Miss_____

Address_____

City_____State_____Zip_____

FC—6/77